ENGLISH
VOCABULARY
MADE EASY

Prof. Shrikant Prasoon

V&S PUBLISHERS

Published by:

V&S PUBLISHERS

F-2/16, Ansari Road, Daryaganj, New Delhi-110002
☎ 011-23240026, 011-23240027 • *Fax:* 011-23240028
Email: info@vspublishers.com • *Website:* www.vspublishers.com

Branch : Hyderabad
5-1-707/1, Brij Bhawan (Beside Central Bank of India Lane)
Bank Street, Koti, Hyderabad - 500 095
☎ 040-24737290
E-mail: vspublishershyd@gmail.com

Follow us on:

For any assistance sms **VSPUB** to **56161**

All books available at **www.vspublishers.com**

© **Copyright:** *V&S PUBLISHERS*
ISBN 978-93-505707-9-1
Edition 2014

Printed at : Unique Colour Carton, New Delhi-110020

Dedication

Dedicated to all the lovers of learning

Who wish to live by and play with words;

And

To all

Who are studying at

Different places;

In different standards

And different subjects

And

To my grandchildren

Tanu Tanvi; Shridhar Chaturvedi,

Prajjwal Stotra; Prakhar Shloka

And Laxmi Stuti.

Publisher's Note

It has been our prime motto and a constant endeavour at the **V&S Publishers** to publish books of **Value** and **Substance** from the time of its inception. With a backlist of **about 350 titles** to our credit, it's a great pleasure to inform all our esteemed readers that we have come up with this altogether exclusive series of books on **English language and its various usage** called the **EXC-EL Series or the Excellent English Learning Series**.

The series contains a set of **four books** on *various usage of* Words and Phrases in English, the significance of Grammar, correct Pronunciation, etc., called *English Grammar And Usage, English Vocabulary made Easy, Improve Your Vocabulary* and *Spoken English* to enhance and enrich your vocabulary, increase your command over the language and make you more confident and fluent in your day to day conversations, written and verbal interactions, etc.

As we are all aware of the fact that English as a language has a rich heritage and a long history. It is believed to have originated from the Anglo-Frisian dialects brought to Britain by the Germanic invaders or settlers from various parts of north-west Germany and the Netherlands. The Modern English language that we speak, read or write today has undergone extensive changes in the Middle Ages and has been completely transformed with a vast and rich vocabulary which is completely different from its origin in the yesteryears. It has become diverse with words and phrases of other languages, like American, French, Spanish, etc., incorporating into this language making it all the more vast and complicated.

The Modern English of today has innumerable **idioms, phrases, proverbs, one-word substitutes, antonyms, synonyms, homophones, homonyms, prefixes, suffixes and acronyms (abbreviations),** all of which have been elaborately discussed in this book. Hence, it is a must read for students of all ages, particularly the school going ones.

Contents

Publisher's Note 5

Preface 9

Know the Words 11

Ways of Learning Words 13

Begin with A Test 16

SECTION-1 : Functional Vocabulary 20

   Chapter 1. **Words & Words** 21

      Countable & Uncountable Noun... 21

      Commonly used Countable & Uncountable Nouns................ 21

      Other Interesting words 22

      Words Commonly Mispronounced... 22

      Words Commonly Misspelt.. 24

      Words Often Misspelt 25

      Words in Plural... 25

      Foreign Words 28

   Chapter 2. **Words and Formation of Words** 32

      Words 32

      Words & Words in English 33

      Formation of Words 34

      Compound Formation.. 34

      Derivation 35

      Back Formation 36

      Duplication 37

      Conversion 38

      Clipping... 38

      Acronyms... 39

      Similes & Metaphors 39

      Blending 40

Word Manufacture.. 40

Multiple Formation... 40

Changes in Formation.. 40

Chapter 3.   Formation of Nouns, Adjectives, Adverbs & Verbs.............. **42**

Formation of Nouns from Verbs... 42

Formation of Abstract Nouns from Concrete Nouns 45

Formation of Adjectives from Nouns 46

Formation of Adjectives from Verbs.. 48

Formation of Adverbs from Adjectives 50

Formation of Verbs from Nouns 50

Formation of Verbs from Adjectives.. 53

Chapter 4.   Comparison... **56**

Comparisons.. 56

Chapter 5.   Collective Nouns.. **58**

Collective Nouns & their Usage 58

Chapter 6.   Singular and Plurals Nouns... **61**

List of Singular & Plural Nouns 61

Chapter 7.   Adjectives.. **65**

List of Adjectives.. 65

Chapter 8.   Verbs.. **68**

List of Verbs 68

Chapter 9.   Miscellaneous... **71**

Adverbs & Conjunctions... 71

Cries of Birds 72

Sounds of Objects... 72

Terms from the Business World 73

Words Related to Battle 75

Common Words from Sanskrit 76

Compound Words... 78

Words used in Pairs 79

Chapter 10.   Double Letters **81**

Chapter 11.   Silent Letters **84**

SECTION-2 : Building Vocabulary.. **87**

Chapter 12.   Prefixes **88**

Chapter 13.   Suffixes **100**

Chapter 14.   Antonyms: Opposites... **117**

Opposite Words...117

Multiple Opposites 120

Chapter 15.   Synonyms: Similar in Meaning **124**

Multiple Synonyms 124

Chapter 16. Homonyms: Homophones **127**
Words that We Generally Confuse 128

Chapter 17. Acronyms **130**

Chapter 18. Abbreviations **132**

Chapter 19. One-word Substitutes **134**
One Word for Many Words **134**
Trades and Professions.. 139
Types of People 142
Government Words 146

Chapter 20. Words of Daily Use **148**
(a) What to Talk about Television? 148
(b) What to Talk about Hair? 150
(c) What to Talk about Food? 151
(d) What to Talk about Good Things or Persons? 151
(e) What to Talk about Persons, Personality and Character? 152
(f) How to Describe the features of a Man? 153
(g) What to Talk about Weather? 154
(h) What to Talk about Beautiful People and Things? 154
(i) What to Talk about Dances and Dancers? 155
(j) What to Talk about Travels?... 155
(k) What to Talk about Air Travel? 156

SECTION 3 : Formal & Informal Words.. **157**

Chapter 21. American English... **158**
Origin of words 162

Chapter 22. Headline English (Newspaper English) **164**
Noun Phrase 164
Noun Strings.. 164
Various Verb Changes 164
Different Types of Newspaper Headlines 165

Chapter 23. Language of Signboard, Notice Board, Ad, etc. **167**
Analysis.. 167
Conclusion 168
Notice Board Writing 168
Characteristics of Notice Board Writing..................................... 169
Writing Good Advertisements 169
What's the Significance of a Good Ad?....................................... 171

Chapter 24. Proverbs, Idioms & Idiomatic Expressions....................... **173**
What is a Proverb? 173

Preface

'*English Vocabulary made Easy*' is a book designed for those who want to enrich their vocabulary; increase their self-awareness in speaking and writing the English language. Correct spelling is fast eroding because of the SMS and Internet language; and to learn the meaning in contextual fashion in a different and effective way without actually reading the meaning or consulting a dictionary.

In '*English Vocabulary made Easy*', the words have been presented in various contexts and in many ways. A number of aspects of learning words have been discussed in detail to help the readers accumulate words, build a strong vocabulary and learn the exact and appropriate use of words for an apt and fluent expression of the language.

How words are formed and how do the words grow? All have been shown by examples. Special attention has been paid for developing the inner sense of words and control over spellings.

After going through the *English Vocabulary made Easy*, readers will feel elated at their progress, and have a clear understanding about the usage of words which will enhance their vision and confidence. The readers will become actively receptive to new words. It is the confidence that counts and the concentration that pays high dividends. *English Vocabulary made Easy* will give both the confidence and concentration.

The book has been aimed to serve both who feel at home in English and those who are alien to the language. It will easily remove some of the inherent psychological difficulties. Those who are afraid of writing, because of lack of exact words and expressions, will feel an inner urge to write as they learn the exact words for describing different things rather than whatever they wish to describe.

For the sake of saving time, there are people who have invented a special language for SMS, Internet, etc, although they know it well that '*Time saved is time spent.*' Its popularity has ruined their knowledge of 'spelling'. When they are employed and are forced to prepare projects by sending reports to their Bosses, they feel shy. This book will shake off that fear and shyness forever.

English Vocabulary made Easy has all the features valuable for the present-day readers who have to communicate something related to the highly untraditional and unfamiliar equipments and the ideas. This will definitely enrich their vocabulary. It will widen their views and attitude; broaden their ideas and their usage of English language making it more appropriate and expressive. Now, it is in your hands to enjoy, utilise and grow enhancing your knowledge with the proper usage of the book. The more you read, the more you can learn to add the different types of words and their usage in your own vocabulary, and this will open new horizons in the form of new and innovative ideas and set a goal for you to find several new words everyday.

Know the Words

1.

*Words are wealth to be accumulated and spent;
They can't come from dictionaries or be taken on rent;
Words must be learnt and used to have a mastery over
them: If idle or unused, the mind marks them absent.*

2.

*As sound and word is life and represents the Creator;
Words gain sacred entity of the orator, writer and the
promoter; Words must be sweet, convincing, right and
righteous: The rough language makes one a devil, killer,
a traitor.*

3.

*Words express emotions thickening or thinning; Ideas
and impressions pure, healthy or sickening; Words are
rich laden with flavour and fragrance: Truthfully, the
words carry and express different and deep meanings.*

4.

*All such words are useless which are not known;
They are non-existent entity if not seen or shown;
They are incomplete for they need voice or hand For
correct sound or writing: growing or grown.*

5.

*Words are steps towards refinement and richness; They
bear and feel the burden of a sincere witness; Different
meanings stand at different layers graded: Unmitigated
stored in their alert, living, inner recess.*

Ways of Learning Words

Learning words is fun, a game, a play. Those who enjoy it learn words more easily. One draws pure pleasure from it. One lives, thinks, talks and writes confidently. Life, tests, exams and problems are not difficult or burden for them. Knowing more words, means possessing more ideas, growing intellectually, with greater accuracy; easy analysis and correct solutions. They enjoy command over words which are readily and timely available to them. Hence, they have ready solutions. In this age of projects and reports, command over written language is a boon. For such men, life is always triumphant and challenging.

There are various ways of learning words:

❏ Many students still prefer the **alphabetical way** of learning words with the help of a **dictionary**. But it takes a lot of time and labour.

❏ Nowadays, the *phonic way of learning words* has become very popular. It is *P nini's way*. The words are learnt through their basic sounds and roots. Though, English is quite an unscientific language, yet through phonetics, the learned men have tried to give a scientific and logical form and shape to its rich vocabulary, and to search out patterns. The meaning too is to be learnt through sounds and through prefixes and suffixes.

❏ The formation of words gets importance in learning them. It is treated as a better and more lucid way to learn words than the alphabetical method.

❏ One can learn words through 'roots' which is the Sanskrit way of learning words. It's more scientific and cultured. Even the meanings are derived through roots and derivatives.

❏ Norman Lewis' book, "Word Power Made Easy" made this way of learning quite popular among the academicians and students. The author takes the root and makes the word grow. He shows the process and establishes the possibilities of meanings: both smoothly and painstakingly.

❏ There is yet another way, known as the Appendix's way or the subject's way. In it, a subject is taken and the words related to that subject are given or collected and learnt. In books, it is given at the end as *Appendices*.

❏ Another interesting way to learn words is through *Prefixes* and *Suffixes*. They give an idea of spellings without learning them by their roots and also give an insight into the meaning of the words. They elucidate and even explain without using many unnecessary words and sentences.

❏ Memorising words, spellings, meanings, forms, and learning their usage are the primary aspects of English language. This is the reason that it takes many precious years of the learners and yet the mastery remains a mirage.

❏ By following the methods mentioned above, one can acquire better understanding, and enjoy quicker and greater command over the usage of the language.

❏ Of course, there are many ways but 'no way out'. All the ways end at a blind lane. When the words are under control, the usage spell the fall. Just by following one particular way, one can't be a master or an expert. If the usage is not underone's control, then apt and appropriate words confuse. That is why most of the writers and orators have their personal vocabulary and work within those limitations. What the users have to do is to win the race under their own limitations and follow mixed ways or all the ways of learning available.

❏ Because the words in English have been borrowed from various languages; from almost all the major languages of the world, it has very few original words. Some claim it to be only 270 and others raise this number to 700. Other words in English are borrowed. It generally flourishes on borrowed wealth.

❏ For shaking off the monotony created by a one-way traffic of learning, adopt and follow each of the ways of learning words to roar past others on the highway of success riding the powerful vehicle of vocabulary; to move freely in the enchanting lanes of words while stepping on and off the uneven footpaths of usage, and in order to cross over the crowded streets of competitions to walk on the rough roads of jobs.

❏ A very intimate relationship with words and a familiarity with their contours, nature and character will grow and keep one in constant contact and touch with numerous of them; the detailed maps and complete sketches that will be in possession of the learners which will give them access to different regions and sub-regions of life. One will be able to know and absorb their essence and enjoy the power.

❏ Use the given words in the book deliberately and constantly in sentences of your own to make them serve your purpose. The words will come to you at your beck and call, the most appropriate ones at the most opportune moments.

❏ One can't achieve perfection, but one can come very close to perfection and get the pleasure out of knowledge, friendship and intimacy with words as reputed poets, writers and orators do.

❏ Mind is a natural computer with the configuration of the highest order. It takes things on its own, stores, retains, classifies and supplies them at the most opportune moments. Let your mind grow freely with utmost pleasure and freedom, while playing with words, their structures, meanings and usage.

❏ This will enable you to take a leisure and confident walk on the uneven; turning; familiar footpaths of a long life.

- ❏ The book, *Words and Words* contains all the ways and provides ample examples to clear the path for the learners so that they can smoothly pass on.

- ❏ Words are the symbols of knowledge to accurate thinking. Most of the successful and intelligent people have the biggest vocabulary.

- ❏ Successful people have greater vocabularies. People who are intellectually alive and successful in the professional world are accustomed to dealing with ideas which come from learning new words.

Begin with A Test

Here are 100 questions. Answer them first. Write your answer on a separate page. Then, check the answers with the answers given at the end of the questions. Don't read the answers before answering the questions. You won't be able to evaluate yourself. Tally your score with the grades given after the answers. You will know where you stand?

Now, take a copy and a pen; and get started.

Choose the correct spellings and tick (✓) them in the table below.

S.N.	a.	b.	c.
1.	Gunia	Guinea	Gunea
2.	Mediterranean	Mediterranian	Medeterranean
3.	Swizerland	Switzerland	Switzarland
4.	Whereever	Whereevar	Wherever
5.	Mercury	Mercary	Marcury
6.	Circumference	Circumferance	Circomference
7.	Adjecent	Adjacent	Aidjacent
8.	Parler	Parlaur	Parlour
9.	Vantilator	Ventilator	Ventilater
10.	Safficient	Sufficient	Sufficiant
11.	Miscellenous	Miscellaneous	Misllaneous
12.	Mantenance	Maintainance	Maintenance
13.	Modelled	Modled	Moddled
14.	Necessity	Necacity	Necesity
15.	Coincide	Coancide	Concide
16.	Bouyant	Buoyent	Boyant
17.	Asserten	Ascertain	Assertain
18.	Autamn	Autumn	Autum
19.	Banquette	Banquett	Bankwet
20.	Benefiscent	Beneficent	Benificial

Choose the correct word in each of the following sentences.

1. She murmured/whispered in her dream.
2. It was a deadly bait/wait.
3. She heard the announcement/warning and was ready to board the plane.
4. I wondered/wandered lonely as a cloud.
5. I visited a wholly/holy place.
6. They are conscious of people's warfare/welfare.
7. They wound/wounded the watch on the tower.
8. A balanced waist/waste gives a good shape.
9. He is earning/yearning for a decent job.
10. The duplicate/triplicate was just like him.
11. He was looking for a vacation/vacancy in the paper.
12. It was valuation/value added tax.
13. That shining vehicle is not important/imported.
14. She engaged a tuition/tutor.
15. He was taken/back to hospital after the accident.
16. He can't show his vacant/empty stomach.
17. The ultimate/urgency was the decisive factor.
18. There was no substitute/substance in him.
19. Technology/mechanics is paying high dividends.
20. Her tamper/temper is a cause of concern for all.
21. The old rule is still in affect/effect.
22. They remained united in averse/adverse conditions.
23. He has no excess/access to the authorities.
24. The book of stories was amended/emended.
25. This book is the best compliment/complement to that one.
26. She has got a pure conscience/consciousness.
27. They all enjoyed the desert/dessert.
28. He faired/fared well in the exam.
29. The dirty water was not potable/portable.
30. The reign/rein was not liked by the people.
31. The decoration was tasty/tasteful.
32. I remembered/recollected her every day.
33. A large number/amount of rice was bought.
34. She was anxious/eager to see him healthy again.
35. Our masons are good artisans/artists.
36. In a month or two, she will be better/well.
37. He is in search of some recruitment/employment.

38. The weather/climate was stormy.
39. Some alterations and editions/additions have been made in this book.
40. He produced written testimony/evidence before the learned judge.

Give a Synonym for each of the following:

1. Proud
2. Peaceful
3. Prohibit
4. Permit
5. Pious
6. Paralyse
7. Pity
8. Plentitude
9. Predecessor
10. Profane
11. Promote
12. Patience
13. Prodigal
14. Preach
15. Precision
16. Premier
17. Prey
18. Primary
19. Prison
20. Private

Give an Antonym for each of the following:

1. Pride
2. Printing
3. Production
4. Progress
5. Prosperity
6. Protection
7. Pleasure
8. Part
9. Pause
10. People
11. Permission
12. Pirated
13. Place
14. Plane
15. Playful
16. Pleasant
17. Pollute
18. Prepaid
19. Paltry
20. Pick

Check Your Answers

Give one mark to each of the correct answer.

1.1

1. Guinea	2. Mediterranean	3. Switzerland	4. Wherever
5. Mercury	6. Circumference	7. Adjacent	8. Parlour
9. Ventilator	10. Sufficient	11. Miscellaneous	12. Maintenance
13. Modelled	14. Necessity	15. Coincide	16. Buoyant
17. Ascertain	18. Autumn	19. Banquet	20. Beneficial

1.2

1. Murmurred	2. Bait	3. Announcement	4. Wandered
5. Holy	6. Welfare	7. Wound	8. Waist
9. Yearning	10. Duplicate	11. Vacancy	12. Value
13. Imported	14. Tutor	15. Taken	16. Empty
17. Urgency	18. Substance	19. Technology	20. Temper
21. Effect	22. Adverse	23. Access	24. Emended
25. Complement	26. Conscience	27. Dessert	28. Fared
29. Potable	30. Rein	31. Tasteful	32. Remembered
33. Amount	34. Eager	35. Artisan	36. Well
37. Employment	38. Weather	39. Additions	40. Evidence

1.3

1. Vain	2. Quiet	3. Forbid	4. Allow
5. Holy	6. Cripple	7. Brief	8. Maximum
9. Precursor	10. Unholy	11. Elevate	12. Forbearance
13. Spendthrift	14. Teach	15. Accuracy	16. Famous
17. Hunt	18. Main	19. Jail	20. Secret

1.4

1. Humility	2. Writing	3. Destruction	4. Retrograde
5. Adversity	6. Desertion	7. Pain	8. Whole
9. Move	10. Animal	11. Denial	12. Original
13. Remove	14. Uneven	15. Sober	16. Disgusting
17. Clean	18. Postpaid	19. Much	20. Throw

Your Score

30 %	Very poor	40 %	Poor
50 %	Average	60 %	Good
70 %	Grand	80 %	Superb

SECTION-1
FUNCTIONAL VOCABULARY

Chapter 1

Words & Words

Countable & Uncountable Nouns

(A)   Nouns can be either be countable or uncountable. Countable nouns are those which can have the word a/an or be used in the plural form. Uncountable nouns are not used with *a* or *an* or in plural form. An example of a countable noun is:-

We got <u>two</u> children, <u>three</u> cats and <u>a</u> dog.

Example of an uncountable noun:-

It was good to get out into the <u>countryside</u> and breathe in some fresh air.

(B)   Sometimes a noun is used uncountably when we are talking about the whole substance or idea, but countably when we are talking about

1.   Recognised containers for things or comparisons.

2.   I prefer <u>tea</u> to coffee and three <u>teas</u> please.

(C)   Some nouns have different meanings when they are used countably or uncountably e.g.

The jewellery box is made of <u>tin</u> (the metal)

There are many <u>tins</u> (metal food containers) lying in the backyard.

(D)   Some nouns that are usually used uncountably can be used countably, but only in the singular form, education, importance, traffic, resistance, knowledge etc.

E.g., she has an exclusive <u>knowledge</u> of property prices in India.

The noun, damage can be used countably, but only in plural form.

She is claiming <u>damages</u> (money paid as compensation) for the injuries caused.

Commonly used Countable & Uncountable Nouns

Countable Nouns: The nouns that can be counted.

men	bags	countries
capitals	players	wickets
gloves	leaves	offices

animals	fruits	vehicles
trees	shops	insects
games	professionals	tablets
sticks	trays	boots
permits	scenes	poems
garments	jerseys	tickets
computers	systems	scholars

Uncountable/Non-countable Nouns: The nouns that can't be counted

water	milk	heat
coolness	flour	sugar
wisdom	rice	vice
tea	ink	coffee
kindness	ugliness	silver
gold	copper	grass
happiness	flood	joy
gladness	goodness	sadness
praise	work	laughter
permission	scenery	clothing
travel	ice	steel
chalk	coal	newness
hope	charity	love

Uncountable Nouns can be changed into Countable Nouns

A piece of work	a loaf of bread	a piece of ice
A piece of advice	a rod of steel	a bar of gold
A brick of silver	a cake of chocolate	a pack of cream
A lump of coal	a piece of news	a heap of flour
A look of kindness	an appearance of sadness	a smile of satisfaction
A herd of elephants	a pack of wolves	a leaf of bread

Other Interesting Words

There are many interesting words in the English language.

1. Queuing is the only word with five vowels in a row.
2. Fashion and cushion are the only words that end in 'Shion'.

Words Commonly Mispronounced

improvement	increase	suicide
inhale	innocent	knowledge

optional	plenty	optimist
ordinarily	initial	logical
partial	execute	antonyms
normal	scarcity	ignorance
parting	exhale	misery
impartial	chauvinism	follower
pessimist	borrow	abnormal
everything	hierarchy	rhythm
chauvinistic	synonym	deteriorate
immodest	marginal	unique
illogical	guilty	incapable
incurable	incompetent	indecision
correct	exhaustible	delirium
decibel	experience	fusion
validity	consistency	conspicuous
decency	dispose	bear
inaction	virtues	patriarch
inequality	reactivated	ingratitude
efficacy	ineffective	inadequate
denture	inadvisable	inorganic
inanimate	insane	inapplicable
inseparable	insincere	intolerant
posture	architecture	inauspicious
incoherent	inconclusive	insufficient
indiscreet	maximise	tranquility
apologize	blacken	encouraging
magnificence	strengthen	industrialisation
fertilization	moisture	inequality
sociology	transplantation	systematic
sympathetic	aggression	machinery
substitution	familiarisation	contribution
electrification	miniature	signature
pronunciation	mammal	professional
regimentation	extension	excessive
contagious	geometrical	figurative

formative	volunteer	moderation
calculator	foliage	figurative
departure	scripture	nurture
creature	gesture	creative

Words Commonly Misspelt

wearily	poultry	appointment
acquiesce	collection	eagerly
tyrant	molest	operation
repentance	equator	consideration
dentist	vegetable	perfectly
sprout	perfectionist	expanse
quarterly	trousers	wages
except	trouble	prepare
impression	stretch	distraction
prevention	refusal	creditor
debtor	defendant	defensive
deficit	different	difficult
diligent	emptiness	plaintiff
examinee	enmity	entrance
economical	elementary	stationary
extravaganza	frugality	exclusion
imperceptible	multiplicity	existence
thunder	throat	palpable
splitting	treasury	fretful
treacherous	audible	commandant
sterilize	stammering	universality
loyalty	niece	perceive
achieve	believe	receive
sieve	deceive	conceive
chief	sufficient	deficient
brief	oriental	retrieve
grief	reign	reindeer
toaster	flour	biscuits
pouring	plough	daisy
howler	threatening	pierce

clamant	wither	windfall
progressive	instrumental	hideous
queue	exclamatory	exemplify
porous	reporter	imitable
guardian	grinder	sapling
changeable	weigh	courageous
believe	inoculate	seize
achieve	apostrophe	protein
grief	weird	yield

Words Often Misspelt

A list of some nonsense words have been listed here. The words are valuable only for their sounds and its peculiarity. The tongue is to be twisted deliberately and with effort in order to pronounce them. Practise them, not for their use in writing but for their impact on speaking, particularly to vex others.

whoostle	labillen	glaphwhup
davitle	phlog	whaff
moomify	gebbuph	whushing
krimicut	yalliry	phat
whinching	dojitate	caget
whull	caph	cyck
wiggle	ciph	caption
wallowow	gyle	negetate
waggle	goak	heng
emphideecoph	ingundermate	henisate
boobillimer	jorojate	bobbledewoop
booching	insissle	graffiti
carvvity	bishy	bithisish
engendist	igness	pissysissy

Words in Plural

Words that have the same form in singular and plural

deer	sheep	fish
salmon	yoke	brace
dozen	score	stone (when denotes weight)
hundred-weight	pice	hundred
thousand		

Exceptions: When 'of' is used; **Examples**: *dozens* of mangoes; *scores* of people; *hundreds* of women, *thousands* of rupees

Words that have two forms in plural but with different meanings

Brother –   a. brothers = sons of same parents

                   b. brethren = members of the same society

cloth –   a. cloths = kinds or pieces of cloth

                   b. clothes = articles of dress

die –   a. dies = stamps for coinage

                   b. dice = small cubes used in games

genius –   a. geniuses = men of genius or talent

                   b. genii = fabulous spirits of the air

index –   a. indexes = Tables of contents

                   b. indices = Signs used in algebra

staff –   a. staves = Sticks or poles

                   b. staffs = Salaried employees taken collectively

shot –   a. shot = Little balls discharged from a gun; attempts to hit by shooting

                   b. shots = Marksmen; photographic recordings

Words that have one meaning in singular and another in plural

Singular	Meaning in singular	Plural	Meaning in plural
advice	counsel	advices	information
beef	flesh of ox	beeves	cattle, bulls and cows
compass	which tells direction	compasses	which draws circle
good	benefit	goods	movable property
iron	a metal	irons	fetters made up of iron
physic	medicine	physics	natural science
return	coming back	returns	profit of an undertaking
vesper	evening	vespers	evening prayers
sand	a matter	sands	a tract of sandy land
force	strength or energy	forces	army; natural forces
air	atmosphere	airs	assumed demeanour

Words that have two meanings in plural

Singular	Meaning in singular	Plural	Meaning in plural
colour	colour	colours	a. kinds of colours
			b. flag of regiment
custom	habit	customs	a. habits

Singular	Meaning in singular	Plural	Meaning in plural
			b. toll or tax
letter	alphabet, epistle	letters	a. alphabet, epistles
			b. learning
pain	suffering	pains	a. sufferings
			b. trouble, care
effect	result	effects	a. results
			b. goods and chattels
manner	mode or way	manners	a. modes or ways
			b. behaviour
number	as in counting	numbers	a. as in counting
			b. metre of poetry
part	portion	parts	a. portions
			b. abilities
spectacle	anything seen	spectacles	a. things seen
			b. glasses to help sight
premise	propositions	premises	a. propositions
			b. houses and grounds
quarter	a fourth part	quarters	a. fourth parts
			b. lodgings

Words which are used in plural

alms	eaves	riches	odds
arms (as weapons)	bellows	fetters	pincers
scissors	tongs	shears	snuffers
breeches	drawers	trappings	trousers
pants	measles	mumps	staggers
gripes	bowels (part of body)	entrails	intestines
annals	dregs	nuptials	obsequies
proceeds	thanks	tidings	downs
wages	auspices	environs	credentials

Words which are used in singular

means	news	innings	Mathematics
Physics	Politics	Economics	Statistics

Foreign Words

(Abbreviations: F for French; I for Italian; L for Latin)

adieu	(F)	= good bye; farewell
A.D.; Anno Domini	(L)	= the year of Christian Era
ADC; aide-de-camp	(F)	= an army officer acting as assistant
ad hoc	(L)	= for special occasion or purpose
ad infinitum	(L)	= infinity; endlessly
ad interim	(L)	= temporary; provisional
ad libitum	(L)	= at pleasure
ad nauseam	(L)	= to a disgusting extent
ad valorem	(L)	= proportionate to the value
aide-memoire	(F)	= note made as an aid to memory
a la, a la mode d	(F)	= after the fashion
a la carte	(F)	= with a stated price for each dish
alias	(L)	= otherwise known as
Alma Mater	(L)	= the bounteous mother
Almunus ptalumini	(L)	= first child, student of an educational institution
a.m., ante meridiem	(L)	= before noon
amende honorable	(F)	= public apology for an offence
a posteriori	(I)	= argument from effect to cause
a priori	(L)	= argument from cause to effect
apropos	(F)	= in the nick of time
Aqua regia	(L)	= royal water; a mixture of nitric acid and hydrochloric acid
art brut	(F)	= primitive art
art modern	(F)	= modern art
avant courier	(F)	= a precursor; one who rides ahead
avant garde	(F)	= cultural pioneers
Ave Maria	(L)	= 'Hail Mary'; opening words of a prayer
beau monde	(L)	= the people of fashion
belles letters	(F)	= literary writing
bona fides	(L)	= genuineness, sincerity
bon not	(F)	= a clever remark
bon vavant	(F)	= fond of luxury and good food
bon voyage	(F)	= a good voyage

circle	(L)	= about
café	(F)	= coffee
carte blanche	(F)	= full power
charge d'affaires	(F)	= diplomat working in place of an ambassador
chauffeur	(F)	= paid driver of a car
compos mentis	(L)	= sound mind
coup de grace	(F)	= the finishing stroke; merciful killing
coup d'etat	(F)	= a sudden change of government by violent means
cuisine	(F)	= kitchen; style of cooking
cul-de-sac	(F)	= the bottom of a bag; a blind alley;
debris	(F)	= piles of rubbish
debut	(F)	= first appearance
de facto	(L)	= in fact
de jure	(L)	= by right; according to law
dramatis personae	(L)	= a list of characters in a play
D.V., Deo volente	(L)	= God willing
e.g., example gratia	(L)	= for example
eldorado	(L)	= the gilded; an imagined country of gold
elite	(F)	= the best people
en block	(F)	= in a lump; in bulk
en masse	(F)	= in a mass; all together
en passant	(F)	= by the way; passing reference
en rapport	(F)	= in sympathy with
en route	(F)	= on the way; bound for
entourage	(F)	= a retinue; a group of friends and attendants
et al/et alia/et alii	(L)	= and other people
etc, ey cetera	(L)	= and the rest
ex libris	(L)	= from the library
ex officio	(L)	= because of one's office
fait acompli	(F)	= an accomplished fact
ibid, ibidem	(L)	= in the same book; at the same place
i.e., id est	(L)	= in other words; that is to say
infra dig, infra dignitatem	(L)	= beneath one's dignity
impasse	(F)	= a blind alley; deadlock
inter alia	(L)	= among other things
laisser-faire	(F)	= the principle of non-interference

laissez-faire	(F)	= in commercial matters by a government
lapsus lingae	(L)	= a slip of tongue
lapsus memoriae	(L)	= a slip of memory
mal a propos; malapropos	(L)	= out of place; in opportune
mala fide	(L)	= bad intention
matinee	(F)	= an afternoon performance
menu	(F)	= a list of dishes that can be served
messieurs	(F)	= gentlemen
modus operandi	(L)	= a way of working
mutatis mutandis	(L)	= with necessary changes in details
N.B., note bene	(L)	= note well
op cit, opera citato	(L)	= in the work cited
parole	(F)	= a promise not to escape
per capita	(L)	= per head
per cent, per centum	(L)	= per hundred
per diem	(L)	= per day
per mensem	(L)	= per month
p.m., *post meridiem*	(L)	= after noon
post mortem	(L)	= after death
prima facie	(L)	= on the face of it
prix fixe	(F)	= a meal offered at a fixed price
pro rata	(L)	= proportionately; in proportion
R.S.V.P., *Respondez s'il vous plait* (F)		= reply, if you please
sine die	(L)	= put off till an unspecified date
sine qua non	(L)	= an indispensable condition or qualification
status quo	(L)	= the existing state of affairs
status quo ante	(L)	= the former state of affairs
sub judice	(L)	= under judgement
sub rosa	(L)	= in strict confidence
table d'note	(F)	= the host's table
terra firma	(L)	= firm earth, dry land
ultra vires	(L)	= beyond the power/authority of a person
v., versus	(L)	= against
via	(L)	= by the route
via media	(L)	= a middle course

vice	(L)	= in place of, in succession to
vice versa	(L)	= the other way round
viva voce	(L)	= oral; orally; with the living voice
viz, videlicet	(L)	= that is to say

Chapter 2

Words and Formation of Words

Words

- ❏ A **word** is a unit of spoken language. It is a written sign which represents an utterance, or a sound.
- ❏ **Words** stand for a language, a saying, a brief conversation, a rumour, a hint or a signal.
- ❏ When used in plural, the meaning of a word extends to a message, a promise, or a declaration.
- ❏ A word becomes a password; a watch word; a war-cry; a set of bits stored and transferred as a single unit of meaning as in computers, etc.
- ❏ As **wordage**, it becomes a text as opposed to pictures; or denotes quality of words or choice of words.
- ❏ When a document is **worded**, it means that it has been expressed in words.
- ❏ The act of expressing in words or phrasing or choice of words is denoted by **wordily** or **wordiness** or **wording**.
- ❏ As an adjective, 'word' becomes **wordish** but is ablative now.
- ❏ A **wordy** man shows **wordiness**, but a **wordless** person remains silent.
- ❏ Those who can't read are called **word-blind** as they suffer from **word-blindness**. In one case, it is alexia and in the other case, it is dyslexia.
- ❏ Like this one; **Words and Words**; a **word-book** is a collection of words for those who are **word-bound**, and are unable to find expression in words.
- ❏ Like them, others too need **word-building**; **word-memory** and **word-play**.
- ❏ There are many **word-processors,** though **word-processing** is a tedious but refined act which makes a man **word-perfect**.
- ❏ **Word-painting** is a sublime art and only **word-painters** can describe something vividly.
- ❏ One should never make a **word salad** as one must not pour out or outpour confusing speech.
- ❏ Instead, we should be **word-smiths**, accomplished user of words.
- ❏ Pun or **wordplay** gives immense pleasure; definitely more than simple **word square**.

- **Word-splitting** is like hair-splitting, and hence is dangerous.
- **A good word** praises or recommends or favourably mentions while a confidential conversation is a **word in one's ears**.
- Some are ready **at a word** and some are **as good as their words**. They can never **break their words**.
- Those who are **word of mouth** are often forced **to eat their words**. They never get **pleasant words** or **fair words** as reply.
- Those who lack **ease in a word** fail to **have a word** with their opponents in time.
- Such men are proved to be men of **many words** which are all meaningless before a man **of few words**. It is neither wise to **take someone at his/her word** nor **to put words in someone's mouth** or **to take words from someone's mouth**.
- The use of the **latest word** shows wisdom, but is not **the last word**.
- They are our Scriptures which are written with capital W and denote the second person in the Trinity.
- In this book, '*Words and Words*', you will have to be verbatim and read **word for word**.
- In literal, literary and symbolic way, a word appears in many forms; gives many meanings and is used in different ways. They are all from Noun to Interjection including Pronoun; Verb; Adverb; Adjectives; Prepositions and Conjunctions. It is both a pleasure and wisdom to collect words and to use them in one's own way or in a traditional way to make them apt and appropriate, and to make one's language effective and impressive.
- Our conversation begins and ends with words.

Words & Words in English

- Obviously, English seems to be one language and Dictionaries contain lakhs of words. But words in English are not from one language, they have been borrowed from almost all the languages of the world: both the languages in current use and obsolete languages.
- Naturally, wherever English is spoken, it has been influenced deeply by the local languages and accent and in turn has influenced the local languages. It is the most natural outcome when two languages come and live together.
- The result is that there is no one English language. There are many: for Example: British English, American English, Canadian English, Australian English, Indian English, Russian English, Chinese English and many more. They have their well established existence: native roots such as: strong native stems, diverse branches, countless native leaves in the form of words, variously coloured flowers and attractive fruits in the form of total effect.
- English has no fixed form and now, it is not the sole property of England. Of course, British English is the base, the parent language but even British English written and spoken in UK is different than that used in the Indian subcontinent. The real reason behind this difference is the publication and distribution of different Dictionaries for the Indian subcontinent and UK, which are not to be sold in UK or vice versa.

❏ English has borrowed not only the words, but also ideas from other languages and literature. It has adopted not only the ways of formation of words, but also the expression of ideas and a bit of Grammar also. Naturally, at many stages and in various ways, words in English are guided by the rules of many languages as they have knowingly or imperceptibly got crept into it. The result is that there are numerous rules and exceptions to the many existent rules in English. The users easily get confused as some follow one rule while the others a different rule.

❏ English is still borrowing from other languages and growing healthy and richer. It is deliberately trying hard to get invincible maturity.

❏ So, there are many processes and different rules of the formation of words in English. Some very popular ones have been discussed in detail in the Morphological Books which are being given here.

Formation of Words

At the very beginning of learning English words, words and words, words through words, words for words, etc, it will be interesting, refreshing, rejuvenating and revealing to learn and know how new words are formed.

Compound Formation

When two or more words are joined together to make a longer word, the process is known as Compound Formation. A compound word can be:

A Noun: Book review, he-man, she-goat, petrol-tank, good-looking, bedroom, silverfish, bluebell, river-bank, open-window, boatman, headquarters, slot-machine, postmark, kitchen-table, hitchhiker, windscreen, film-screen, grounds-man, dark-room, flying-machine, dancing-girl, earthquake, waiting-list, driving-license,

A Pronoun: Myself, yourself, themselves, ourselves, oneself, herself, anybody, somebody, no-one

An Adjective: Oversensitive, milk-white, age-old, bottle-green, breathtaking, trustworthy, life-giving, fact-finding, ocean-going, heartfelt, easy going, hardworking, bird-watching, car-driving, airsick, watertight, fireproof, tragic-comic,

A Verb: Overtake, upset, dry-clean, ill-treat,

An Adverb: Somewhere, anywhere, everywhere, nowhere, whenever, wherever

A Preposition: Into, up to, within,

A Conjunction: Whenever, however, nevertheless

An Interjection: Hey-ho, high-ho, hay-ho, hi-ho,

Formation with Subject + Object: Oil-well, silk-worm, firing-squad, goldmine, honeybee, textile-mill, tear-gas,

Formation with Subject + Verb: Sunrise, landslide, bee-sting, day-break, heart-break, headache, stomachache, toothache, heart-beat, machine-washing, dog-watch, bird-watching, nose-bleeding,

Subject + Complement: Software, women-novelist, windmill, motor-cycle, gas-cooker, boy-husband, girl-friend, goldmine, frogman, blueprint, high-chair, boy-friend, teaspoon, teatime, safety-clutch, safety-bolt, fast-food, chessboard, notice-board, he-man, cap-opener, pop-singer, coffee-mug, goldfish, man-servant

Verb + Object: Book review, house-keeping, pickpocket, haircut, sun worship, word formation, call centre, blood test, book post, sightseeing, letter writing, birth control, handshake, bloodshed, painkiller, hold-all, cut-throat

Verb + Adverbial Particle: Dining room, sitting space, night porter, church going, sleepwalking, home work, shadow boxing, night-flight, dancehall, hiding place, plaything, search light, playground, gun fight, fist fight, walking-stick, grindstone, handwriting, baking powder, fall out, dropout, cutout, clipboard, living room

Like *Bahubrihi Samās* in Samskrit and Hindi, now in English also when two words join together and tale altogether a new meaning, they are called **Bahubrihi Compounds:**

cut-throat, heart-throb, pick pocket, hold all, scarecrow, highbrow, birdbrain, breakfast, loud mouth, block head, skinhead, fat head, pot belly, paperback, butter fingers, heavyweight, hard hat, blue stocking, pale face, redcap

Verb + Object: Life giving, life saving, fact finding, nerve stimulating self defeating, self justifying, heart breaking, nose bleeding, blood shedding

Verb + Adverbial Particle: Machine-made, hand-made, home-made, country-made, sun-tanned, everlasting, well-behaved, etc

Adjective + Completive to a Pronoun: Carefree, tax free, colour blind, duty free, blood-thirsty

Modifier + Adjective: Blood red, stone cold, evergreen, ice-cold, paper thin, sea-green, nut brown, brick red, rock hard, milk white, bitter sweet, bluish green, bluish black, reddish brown, Roman-Catholic, psycho linguistic, bitter sweet, English-Hindi Dictionary, overactive, overmodest, underdeveloped, under trial

Adjective + Adjective: Indo-American Agreement, Japanese American Treaty, Indo-Chinese Border, Indo-Sri Lankan Pact, Inter School Tournament, etc

Derivation

When a new word is formed by adding a **Prefix or Suffix** to a base or by inserting an Infix into a root, it is called *Derivation*. The following are the examples of the three ways:

Pre-fixation: Asleep, anteroom, unhappy, decentralise, abuse, abstract, asleep, unhappy, decentralize, abuse, abnormal.

Auto (self) automatic, autobiography

Circum (aloud) circumstance, circumferences

Dis (apart) disjoin, disable, dislocate

Ex (out of) extract, extension

Extra (beyond) extraordinary, extravagant

De (down) descend, dethrone, demarcate

For (thoroughly) forgive, borbear, forlorn

Fore (before) forego, forecast, foretell

Hyper (beyond) hypercritical, hypertension, hyperbole

Homo (like) homogenous, homophone, homograph

In (into written) inside, indoor, inland

Mis (wrongly) mislead, misspelt, mistaken

Mal (bad) malpractice, malnutrition

Post (after) postpaid, postpone, postdated

Pre (before) pre-requisite, prehistoric, predict

Semi (half) semicolon, semicircle, semi furnished

Sub (under) subordinate, subdivision, subdue

Trans (across) transform, transmit, transport

The above derivatives are called secondary derivatives using prefixes.

Formation of Secondary Suffixes

1. Ness – stiffness, boldness, smartness
2. Hood – childhood, womanhood, boyhood
3. Ling – duckling, seedling, sibling
4. Ship – fellowship, friendship, relationship
5. Ary – library, dispensary, honourary
6. Age – bondage, wastage, blockage
7. Tude – attitude, multitude, solitude, gratitude
8. Mony – testimony, alimony, matrimony
9. Ed – talented, tested, learned
10. Some – handsome, wholesome, quauelsome
11. Ish – reddish, foolish, rubbish
12. Less – useless, hopeless, careless
13. Ly – solely, likely, cowardly, bravely
14. Ate – fortunate, salivate, cultivate captivate
15. En – frighten, sharpen, darten

Suffixation: player, novelist, booklet, greatly, kindness, friendship, childhood, manhood

In-fixation: The oft quoted example is from Shaw's Pygmalion: abso-blooming-lutely. Another example is: Morphology

Back Formation

When a new word is formed by deleting the **Suffix** or some letters from the end of a word, it is called *Back Formation*. Many words have been formed in this way:

Chain smoking	chain smoke	Baby sitter	baby sit
Editor	edit	Burglar	burgle

Television	televise	Gate-crasher	gate-crash
Sleep walking	sleep walk	Cross reference	cross refer
Lip reading	lip read	Dry cleaning	dry clean
Enthusiasm	enthuse	Housekeeper	house keep
Refusal	refuse	Procession	process
Type writer	type write	Handwriting	hand write
Back-biter	back-bite	Interception	intercept

Duplication

Sometimes, new words are formed by repeating an item with a change in the initial consonant or with a change in the medial vowel or by repeating the word. It is known as *Duplication*. They are also called *Rhyming Compounds* as they are compounded by two rhyming words.

Change in the Initial Consonant:

Hocus-pocus;	hotchpotch;	hobnob;	hustle-bustle;
Hanky-panky;	helter-skelter;	higgledy-piggledy;	hurly-burly;
Gorgy-porgy;	mumbo-jumbo;	teeny-weeny;	roly-poly;
Nitty-gritty;	nifty-thrifty;	cuckoo;	rat-a-tat;
Hodge-podge;	bow-wow;	utterly-bitterly;	willy-nilly;
Tit-bit;	nit-wit;	niminy-piminy;	pell-mell
Rat-tat;			

These words are very similar to the rhyming compounds, but are not quite compounds in the English language because the second element is not really a word case it is just a nonsense item added to the root word, to form a rhyme in each case – e.g.

Higgledy – piggledy

Tootsie – loortsie

This formation process is associated in English with child talk (and talk addressed to children) technically called hypocoristic

Language – Examples

Bunnie – wunnie

Henny – penny

Snuggly – porgie

Piggie – wiggie

Changing the Medial Vowel:

flip flap	wishy-washy	dilly-dally	rift raft
tick-tock	riff-raff	zigzag	tittle-tattle

flim-flam	ping-pong	sing-sang	ding-dong
see-saw	flip-flop	itsy-bitsy	chit-chat
nick-nack	niddle-noddle	topsy-turvy	wishy-washy
pitter-patter			

By repeating the word:

bye-bye	fifty-fifty	goody-goody	pooh-pooh
knock-knock	bang-bang	choo-choo	din-din

Conversion

When a word is used either as different parts of speech or in different context or with variation in meaning, it is called **Conversion**. It can be partially converted or completely converted.

sweety palms, palmed the ball, cut finger, tax cut

Clipping

When a word is made smaller without any change in meaning or grammatical class, it is known as *Clipping*. In it, either the initial part is retained or the final part or syllable/syllables or the middle part is retained.

When the initial part of the original word is retained:

brassiere	bra	professor	prof .
microphone	mike	advertisement	ad
photograph	photo	stereophonic	stereo
laboratory	lab	examination	exam
pornography	prono	vegetarian	veg
memorandum	memo	non-vegetarian	non-veg

When the final part of the original word is retained:

telephone	phone
aeroplane	plane
Ominibus	bus

When the middle part of the original word or the final 's' is retained:

influenza	flu
refrigerator	fridge
pyjmas	jams
spectacles	specs
mathematics	maths
diggings	digs

Acronyms

A word composed of the initial letters of a group of words, particularly the name of a company or an association, is called *acronym* or *acronymy*.

When acronyms are pronounced as words:

| UNESCO | NATO | BASIC | IRAC | Laser | Radar |

When acronyms are pronounced as letters:

| EEC | MIT | VIP | BBC | YMCA | AIR |
| DDC | MCD | PMO | WHO | UNO | DDA |

When acronyms are formed with letters taken from the same word:

| TB | TV |

Similes and Metaphors

A **simile** is where two things are directly compared because they share a common feature. The words AS and LIKE are used to compare two words. Eg. As cold AS a dog's nose.

A **metaphor** also compares two things, but it does so more directly WITHOUT using as or like. Eg. **The shop was little gold-mine**.

Exercises

I. Copy these sentences into your note book. At the end of each sentence, write in brackets whether the sentence is an example of a *metaphor* or *simile*.

Eg. The clouds were fluffy *like* cotton wool. (SIMILE)

1. As slippery as an eel.
2. Arnie was a man-mountain.
3. He was a lion in battle.
4. She is as pretty as a picture.
5. The striker was a goal machine.
6. The torch lit up the room as if the sun had risen early.
7. The moon was a misty shadow.
8. My friend has a face like a bag of spanners.

II. Now you are going to make up similes of your own by copying and finishing these sentences.

For example:

1. As good **as** gold
2. As heavy as
3. As cold as
4. As hard as
5. She had skin like a
6. As cool as
7. As quick as

8. He was slow like

9. Slippery like a

Blending

When a new word is formed by combining the meaning and sound of two words, the process is known as *blending*. For example:

Oxebridge	Eurasia	Smog	motel	brunch
Interpol	telecast	heliport	helipad	

Word Manufacture

When any acceptable sequence of sound is arbitrarily selected to make a new word, it is called Word manufacture. For example:

Kodak	Exhilo	Quack	Finnegans
Wake			

Multiple Formation

The formation of a new word by applying two processes of word formation, is known as *Multiple Formation*. For example:

hanky	comfy	pinny	undies
nighty	poromeric		

Changes in Formation

When suffixes are added: When suffixes are added to a word, some changes occur, i.e., the 'y' of 'y' ending words/verbs changes into 'I'. For example:

ally	alliance	apply	application
carry	carriage	qualify	qualification
marry	marriage	try	trial
envy	envious	deny	denial

10. **Changes in "Y" ending Adjectives**: Similar changes occur in 'y' ending Adjectives also. For example:

Adjectives	Adverbs	Nouns
busy	busily	business
easy	easily	easiness
heavy	heavily	heaviness
happy	happily	happiness
lucky	luckily	luckiness
ready	readily	readiness
steady	steadily	steadiness

11. **Change or no change**: In some cases, the final 'e' is either dropped or there is no change. For example:

approve   approval

refuse   refusal

betray   betrayal

Chapter 3

Formation of Nouns, Adjectives, Adverbs & Verbs

Formation of Nouns from Verbs

Verbs		Nouns	Verbs		Nouns
Abound	⇨	Abundance	Attain	⇨	Attainment
Admit	⇨	Admission	Announce	⇨	Announcement
Apply	⇨	Application	Advise	⇨	Advice
Attract	⇨	Attraction	Abide	⇨	Abode
Add	⇨	Addition	Apologise	⇨	Apology
Arrange	⇨	Arrangement	Belong	⇨	Belongings
Adopt	⇨	Adoption	Bear	⇨	Birth
Agree	⇨	Agreement	Believe	⇨	Belief
Amend	⇨	Amendment	Beat	⇨	Beating
Arrive	⇨	Arrival	Betray	⇨	Betrayal
Approve	⇨	Approval	Behave	⇨	Behaviour
Assist	⇨	Assistance	Bless	⇨	Blessing
Allot	⇨	Allotment	Bind	⇨	Bound, Bond
Amuse	⇨	Amusement	Break	⇨	Breach
Amaze	⇨	Amazement	Built	⇨	Building
Act	⇨	Action	Carry	⇨	Carriage
Attend	⇨	Attendance	Choose	⇨	Choice
Affect	⇨	Affection	Conceal	⇨	Concealment
Associate	⇨	Association	Collect	⇨	Collection
Assure	⇨	Assurance	Complete	⇨	Completion

Verbs		Nouns	Verbs		Nouns
Commit	⇨	Commitment	Grow	⇨	Growth
Converse	⇨	Conversation	Handle	⇨	Hand
Connect	⇨	Connection	Hate	⇨	Hatred
Compel	⇨	Compulsion	Heal	⇨	Health
Decide	⇨	Decision	Injure	⇨	Injury
Deny	⇨	Denial	Insure	⇨	Insurance
Deceive	⇨	Deception	Intend	⇨	Intention
Defy	⇨	Defiance	Invent	⇨	Invention
Deliver	⇨	Delivery	Know	⇨	Knowledge
Destroy	⇨	Destruction	Lend	⇨	Loan
Discover	⇨	Discovery	Learn	⇨	Learning
Divide	⇨	Division	Liberate	⇨	Liberty
Do	⇨	Deed	Live	⇨	Life
Draw	⇨	Drawing	Lose	⇨	Loss
Dismiss	⇨	Dismissal	Marry	⇨	Marriage
Eat	⇨	Eatable	Move	⇨	Motion
Elect	⇨	Election	Move	⇨	Movement
Exceed	⇨	Excess	Mean	⇨	Meaning
Expel	⇨	Expulsion	Meet	⇨	Meeting
Exist	⇨	Existence	Memorise	⇨	Memory
Extend	⇨	Extension	Merry	⇨	Merriment
Excel	⇨	Excellence	Narrate	⇨	Narration
Fail	⇨	Failure	Obey	⇨	Obedience
Feed	⇨	Food	Oblige	⇨	Obligation
Float	⇨	Fleet	Occupy	⇨	Occupation
Flow	⇨	Flood	Offend	⇨	Offence
Fly	⇨	Flight	Officiate	⇨	Official
Furnish	⇨	Furniture	Oppose	⇨	Opposition
Gay	⇨	Gaiety	Pass	⇨	Passage
Give	⇨	Gift	Perform	⇨	Performance
Go	⇨	Gait	Practise	⇨	Practice
Grieve	⇨	Grief	Pretend	⇨	Pretention
Guard	⇨	Guardian	Prevent	⇨	Prevention

Verbs		Nouns	Verbs		Nouns
Predict	⇨	Prediction	Seize	⇨	Seizure
Produce	⇨	Production	Sit	⇨	Seat
Produce	⇨	Product	Slay	⇨	Slaughter
Prove	⇨	Proof	Steal	⇨	Stealth
Quote	⇨	Quotation	Strive	⇨	Strife
Receive	⇨	Reception	Strike	⇨	Stroke
Receive	⇨	Receipt	Succeed	⇨	Success
Rely	⇨	Reliance	Teach	⇨	Teaching
Resolve	⇨	Resolution	Tell	⇨	Tale
Respond	⇨	Response	Try	⇨	Trial
Run	⇨	Race			

Formation of Nouns from Adjectives

Adjectives		Nouns	Adjectives		Nouns
Able	⇨	Ability	Empty	⇨	Emptiness
Active	⇨	Activity	Equal	⇨	Equality
Angry	⇨	Anger	False	⇨	Falsehood
Anxious	⇨	Anxiety	Famous	⇨	Fame
Bold	⇨	Boldness	Few	⇨	Fewness
Brave	⇨	Bravery	Fond	⇨	Fondness
Brilliant	⇨	Brilliance	Frail	⇨	Frailty
Brief	⇨	Brevity	Gallant	⇨	Gallantry
Bust	⇨	Business	Good	⇨	Goodness
Calm	⇨	Calmness	Grand	⇨	Grandness
Certain	⇨	Certainty	Hard	⇨	Hardness
Civil	⇨	Civility	Happy	⇨	Happiness
Coward	⇨	Cowardice	High	⇨	Height
Curious	⇨	Curiosity	Hot	⇨	Heat
Dear	⇨	Dearness	Human	⇨	Humanity
Deep	⇨	Depth	Humble	⇨	Humility
Dense	⇨	Density	Just	⇨	Justice
Dirty	⇨	Dirt	Idle	⇨	Idleness
Distant	⇨	Distance	Ignorant	⇨	Ignorance

Adjectives		Nouns	Adjectives		Nouns
Inferior	⇨	Inferiority	Rigid	⇨	Rigidity
Keen	⇨	Keenness	Rival	⇨	Rivalry
Kind	⇨	Kindness	Royal	⇨	Royalty
Lame	⇨	Lameness	Rude	⇨	Rudeness
Local	⇨	Locality	Short	⇨	Shortage
Long	⇨	Length	Silent	⇨	Silence
Loyal	⇨	Loyalty	Strong	⇨	Strength
Mean	⇨	Meanness	Stupid	⇨	Stupidity
Moist	⇨	Moisture	Timid	⇨	Timidity
Mortal	⇨	Mortality	True	⇨	Truthful
Necessary	⇨	Necessity	Ugly	⇨	Ugliness
New	⇨	Newness	Urgent	⇨	Urgency
Noble	⇨	Nobility	Vacant	⇨	Vacancy
Obedient	⇨	Obedience	Vain	⇨	Vanity
One	⇨	Oneness	Various	⇨	Variety
Pious	⇨	Piety	Weak	⇨	Weakness
Perfect	⇨	Perfection	Warm	⇨	Warmth
Poor	⇨	Poverty	Wet	⇨	Wetness
Proud	⇨	Pride	Wide	⇨	Width
Quick	⇨	Quickness	Wise	⇨	Wisdom
Real	⇨	Reality	Young	⇨	Youth
Red	⇨	Redness			

Formation of Abstract Nouns from Concrete Nouns

Concrete Noun		Abstract Noun	Concrete Noun		Abstract Noun
Agent	⇨	Agency	Child	⇨	Childhood
Boy	⇨	Boyhood	Coward	⇨	Cowardice
Bond	⇨	Bondage	Enemy	⇨	Enmity
Broker	⇨	Brokerage	Friend	⇨	Friendship
Coin	⇨	Coinage	Infant	⇨	Infancy
Father	⇨	Fatherhood	Man	⇨	Manhood
Hero	⇨	Heroism	Martyr	⇨	Martyrdom

Concrete Noun	Abstract Noun	Concrete Noun	Abstract Noun
Author	⇨ Authorship	Mother	⇨ Motherhood
King	⇨ Kingship	Slave	⇨ Slavery
Owner	⇨ Ownership	Servant	⇨ Service
Patriot	⇨ Patriotism	Thief	⇨ Theft
Pilgrim	⇨ Pilgrimage	Witch	⇨ Witchcraft
Priest	⇨ Priesthood	Widow	⇨ Widowhood
Robber	⇨ Robbery	Woman	⇨ Womanhood

Formation of Adjectives from Nouns

Nouns	Adjectives	Nouns	Adjectives
Accident	⇨ Accidental	Colony	⇨ Colonial
Air	⇨ Airy	Class	⇨ Classical
Anger	⇨ Angry	Class	⇨ Classic
Advantage	⇨ Advantageous	Cat	⇨ Canine
Affection	⇨ Affectionate	Cloud	⇨ Cloudy
Attention	⇨ Attentive	Clerk	⇨ Clerical
Ancestor	⇨ Ancestral	Crime	⇨ Criminal
Angle	⇨ Angular	Coward	⇨ Cowardly
Age	⇨ Aged	Charm	⇨ Charming
Advice	⇨ Advisable	Day	⇨ Daily
Asia	⇨ Asian	Diligence	⇨ Diligent
Bride	⇨ Bridal	Drama	⇨ Dramatic
Book	⇨ Bookish	Dust	⇨ Dusty
Bush	⇨ Bushy	Ease	⇨ Easy
Black	⇨ Blackish	Essence	⇨ Essential
Boy	⇨ Boyish	Face	⇨ Facial
Burden	⇨ Burdensome	Faith	⇨ Faithful
Care	⇨ Carefree	Father	⇨ Fatherly
Cheer	⇨ Cheerful	Fear	⇨ Fearless
Cheer	⇨ Cheerless	Fear	⇨ Fearful
Circle	⇨ Circular	Friend	⇨ Friendly
Ceremony	⇨ Ceremonial	Harm	⇨ Harmful

Nouns		Adjectives	Nouns		Adjectives
College	⇨	Collegiate	Harm	⇨	Harmless
Hero	⇨	Heroic	Odour	⇨	Odorous
Hour	⇨	Hourly	Picture	⇨	Picturesque
Honour	⇨	Honorable	Policy	⇨	Politic
Ice	⇨	Icy	Pride	⇨	Proud
Injury	⇨	Injurious	Prose	⇨	Prosaic
Influence	⇨	Influential	Poetry	⇨	Poetic
Judge	⇨	Judicial	Pity	⇨	Pitiful
Jealousy	⇨	Jealous	Pity	⇨	Pitiless
Knot	⇨	Knotty	Price	⇨	Precious
Logic	⇨	Logical	Proverb	⇨	Proverbial
Labour	⇨	Laborious	Prejudice	⇨	Prejudicial
Leaf	⇨	Leafy	Practice	⇨	Practical
Line	⇨	Lineal	Question	⇨	Questionable
Lustre	⇨	Lustrous	Quarrel	⇨	Quarrelsome
Man	⇨	Manly	Quarter	⇨	Quarterly
Mercy	⇨	Merciful	Rain	⇨	Rainy
Might	⇨	Mighty	Red	⇨	Reddish
Miser	⇨	Miserly	Relation	⇨	Relative
Merit	⇨	Meritorious	Rose	⇨	Rosy
Mind	⇨	Mental	Smoke	⇨	Smoky
Moment	⇨	Momentary	Solitude	⇨	Solitary
Minister	⇨	Ministerial	Star	⇨	Starry
Money	⇨	Monetary	Sun	⇨	Sunny
Myth	⇨	Mythical	Skill	⇨	Skilful
Name	⇨	Nameless	Snow	⇨	Snowy
Navy	⇨	Naval	Sorrow	⇨	Sorrowful
Needy	⇨	Needy	Space	⇨	Spacious
Neighbour	⇨	Neighbourly	Sympathy	⇨	Sympathetic
Neuter	⇨	Neutral	Time	⇨	Timely
Night	⇨	Nightly	Type	⇨	Typical
Number	⇨	Numeral	Telegraph	⇨	Telegraphic
One	⇨	Only	Terror	⇨	Terrific

Nouns		Adjectives	Nouns		Adjectives
Oil	⇨	Oily	Terror	⇨	Terrible
Thorn	⇨	Thorny	War	⇨	Warlike
Use	⇨	Useful	Woman	⇨	Womanly
Use	⇨	Useless	Wind	⇨	Windy
Verb	⇨	Verbal	Worth	⇨	Worthy
Virtue	⇨	Virtuous	Year	⇨	Yearly
Valour	⇨	Valiant	Youth	⇨	Youthful

Formation of Adjectives from Verbs

Verbs		Adjectives	Verbs		Adjectives
Admire	⇨	Admirable	Love	⇨	Lovable
Agree	⇨	Agreeable	Move	⇨	Movable
Attain	⇨	Attainable	Offend	⇨	Offensive
Avoid	⇨	Avoidable	Obey	⇨	Obedient
Believe	⇨	Believable	Please	⇨	Pleasant
Boast	⇨	Boastful	Please	⇨	Pleasing
Compare	⇨	Comparable	Promise	⇨	Promising
Continue	⇨	Continuous	Rely	⇨	Reliable
Charge	⇨	Chargeable	Revenge	⇨	Revengeful
Collect	⇨	Collective	Repair	⇨	Repairable
Consider	⇨	Considerable	Shine	⇨	Shining
Divide	⇨	Divisible	Slip	⇨	Slippery
Excite	⇨	Excitable	Sleep	⇨	Sleepy
Endure	⇨	Endurable	Talk	⇨	Talkative
Help	⇨	Helpful	Thank	⇨	Thankful
Help	⇨	Helpless	Thank	⇨	Thankless
Love	⇨	Lovely	Trouble	⇨	Troublesome

EXERCISES

Choose the correct Adjectives and fill in the blanks to make meaningful phrases.

notable	novel	numerical
national	nuptial	noble
nimble	necessary	nightly
navigable	next	normal
noxious	negative	nitric
negligent	nervous	neutral
nutritious	noisy	

1. A man of _____ birth
2. A film show twice _____
3. The _____ best
4. The_____
5. _____speakers
6. _____ gases
7. _____ ideas
8. _____ food
9. Happiness
10. Symbols
11. Children
12. Acid
13. as_____ as a goat
14. _____territory
15. Suffering from _____ breakdown
16. _____ of duties
17. _____ virtue
18. _____ condition
19. _____ to health
20. A_____ theatre

Formation of Adverbs from Adjectives

Adjectives		Adverbs	Adjectives		Adverbs
Attentive	⇨	Attentively	Regular	⇨	Regularity
Bad	⇨	Badly	Quick	⇨	Quickly
Brave	⇨	Bravely	Sure	⇨	Surely
Bright	⇨	Brightly	Strong	⇨	Strongly
Comfort	⇨	Comfortably	Soft	⇨	Softly
Deep	⇨	Deeply	Sincere	⇨	Sincerely
Gentle	⇨	Gently	Successful	⇨	Successfully
Happy	⇨	Happily	Willing	⇨	Willingly
Loving	⇨	Lovingly	Urgent	⇨	Urgently
Merry	⇨	Merrily	Forceful	⇨	Forcefully
Neat	⇨	Neatly	Joyful	⇨	Joyfully
Obedient	⇨	Obediently	Tasteful	⇨	Tastefully
Perfect	⇨	Perfectly			

Formation of Verbs from Nouns

Nouns		Verbs	Nouns		Verbs
Advice	⇨	Advise	Breath	⇨	Breathe
Air	⇨	Aerate	Bath	⇨	Bathe
Abatement	⇨	Abate	Beginning	⇨	Begin
Access	⇨	Accede	Bitter	⇨	Embitter
Able	⇨	Enable	Bold	⇨	Embolden
Apology	⇨	Apologise	Brood	⇨	Breed
Admiration	⇨	Admire	Capital	⇨	Capitalise
Attention	⇨	Attentive	Colony	⇨	Colonise
Appearance	⇨	Appear	Civil	⇨	Civilise
Absorption	⇨	Absorb	Camp	⇨	Encamp
Authority	⇨	Authorise	Cloth	⇨	Clothe
Body	⇨	Embody	Clean	⇨	Cleanse
Base	⇨	Debase	Circle	⇨	Encircle
Blood	⇨	Bleed	Courage	⇨	Encourage
Bath	⇨	Bathe	Company	⇨	Accompany
Bed	⇨	Embed	Clear	⇨	Clarify
Beauty	⇨	Beautify	Cage	⇨	Encage

Nouns		Verbs	Nouns		Verbs
Class	⇨	Classify	Firm	⇨	Confirm
Criticism	⇨	Criticise	Full	⇨	Fill
Custom	⇨	Accustom	Foul	⇨	Befoul
Centre	⇨	Centralise	Famine	⇨	Famish
Congratulation	⇨	Congratulate	Fertile	⇨	Fertilise
Certain	⇨	Ascertain	Fresh	⇨	Refresh
Character	⇨	Characterise	Fruit	⇨	Fructify
Claim	⇨	Acclaim	False	⇨	Falsify
Danger	⇨	Endanger	Fright	⇨	Frighten
Drop	⇨	Drip	Fraud	⇨	Defraud
Deep	⇨	Deepen	Frost	⇨	Freeze
Detention	⇨	Detain	Glory	⇨	Glorify
Dense	⇨	Condense	Grass	⇨	Graze
Departure	⇨	Depart	Generation	⇨	Generate
Dear	⇨	Endear	Glad	⇨	Gladden
Deity	⇨	Deify	Gold	⇨	Gild
Dew	⇨	Bedew	Glass	⇨	Glaze
Error	⇨	Err	Game	⇨	Gamble
Equal	⇨	Equalise	Guile	⇨	Beguile
Entry	⇨	Enter	Hand	⇨	Handle
Explanation	⇨	Explain	Head	⇨	Behead
Example	⇨	Exemplify	Humble	⇨	Humiliate
Electricity	⇨	Electrify	Half	⇨	Halve
Economy	⇨	Economise	Height	⇨	Heighten
Fool	⇨	Befool	Haste	⇨	Hasten
Force	⇨	Enforce	Habit	⇨	Habituate
Food	⇨	Feed	Hard	⇨	Harden
Fame	⇨	Defame	Health	⇨	Heal
Fat	⇨	Fatten	Heir	⇨	Inherit
Flight	⇨	Fly	Harmony	⇨	Harmonise
Fine	⇨	Refine	Horror	⇨	Horrify
Friend	⇨	Befriend	Injury	⇨	Injure

Nouns		Verbs	Nouns		Verbs
Invention	⇨	Invent	Poor	⇨	Impoverish
Idol	⇨	Idolize	Peace	⇨	Pacify
Imagination	⇨	Imagine	Prison	⇨	Imprison
Intention	⇨	Intend	Population	⇨	Populate
Justice	⇨	Justify	Prevention	⇨	Prevent
Joy	⇨	Enjoy	Popular	⇨	Popularise
Knee	⇨	Kneel	Person	⇨	Personify
Little	⇨	Belittle	Publisher	⇨	Publish
Life	⇨	Live	Practice	⇨	Practise
Long	⇨	Lengthen	Peril	⇨	Imperil
Large	⇨	Enlarge	Port	⇨	Import, Export
Lion	⇨	Lionize	Pure	⇨	Purify
Light	⇨	Lighten	Profession	⇨	Profess
Light	⇨	Enlighten	Right	⇨	Rectify
Mass	⇨	Amass	Revolution	⇨	Revolve
Movement	⇨	Move	Rare	⇨	Rarify
Mad	⇨	Madden	Red	⇨	Redden
Moist	⇨	Moisten	Relation	⇨	Relate
Memory	⇨	Memorise	Real	⇨	Realise
Mind	⇨	Remind	Rich	⇨	Enrich
Monopoly	⇨	Monopolise	Sure	⇨	Ensure
Noble	⇨	Ennoble	Signal	⇨	Signify
Nest	⇨	Nestle	Service	⇨	Serve
Nation	⇨	Nationalise	Sympathy	⇨	Sympathise
New	⇨	Renew	Speech	⇨	Speak
Nature	⇨	Naturalise	Simple	⇨	Simplify
Necessity	⇨	Necessitate	Success	⇨	Succeed
Opposition	⇨	Oppose	Sale	⇨	Sell
Objection	⇨	Object	Strength	⇨	Strengthen
Office	⇨	Officiate	Short	⇨	Shorten
Observation	⇨	Observe	Society	⇨	Associate
Patron	⇨	Patronise	Safety	⇨	Save

Nouns		Verbs	Nouns		Verbs
Sweet	⇨	Sweeten	Tale	⇨	Tell
Slave	⇨	Enslave	Tomb	⇨	Entomb
Snare	⇨	Ensnare	Title	⇨	Entitle
Suggestion	⇨	Suggest	Unity	⇨	Unify, Unite
Siege	⇨	Besiege	Vacancy	⇨	Vacate
Sermon	⇨	Sermonise	Vapour	⇨	Evaporate
Shelf	⇨	Shelve	Verse	⇨	Versify
Spark	⇨	Sparkle	Vice	⇨	Vitiate
Substance	⇨	Substantiate	Vigour	⇨	Invigorate
System	⇨	Systematise	Victim	⇨	Victimise
Trial	⇨	Try	Width	⇨	Widen
Table	⇨	Tabulate	Weak	⇨	Weaken
Throne	⇨	Enthrone, Dethrone	Web	⇨	Weave

Formation of Verbs from Adjectives

Adjectives		Verbs	Adjectives		Verbs
Able	⇨	Enable	Low	⇨	Lower
Abundant	⇨	Abound	Moist	⇨	Moisten
Base	⇨	Debase	Proper	⇨	Appropriate
Bitter	⇨	Embitter	Pure	⇨	Purify
Bold	⇨	Embolden	Public	⇨	Publish
Broad	⇨	Broaden	Quiet	⇨	Quieten
Cheap	⇨	Cheapen	Sick	⇨	Sicken
Clean	⇨	Clarity	Special	⇨	Specialise
Dark	⇨	Darken	Solid	⇨	Consolidate
Familiar	⇨	Familiarise	Stupid	⇨	Stupefy
Feeble	⇨	Enfeeble	Timid	⇨	Intimidate
Fertile	⇨	Fertilise	Thick	⇨	Thicken
Firm	⇨	Confirm, Affirm	Venerable	⇨	Venerate
Hale	⇨	Heal	White	⇨	Whiten
Large	⇨	Enlarge	Wide	⇨	Widen
Liquid	⇨	Liquidate			

Choose the correct words from the following table and fill in the blanks.

hesitate	rejuvenate	penetrated	
mandate	gradate	terminated	
motivate	migrated	germinate	
reanimated	mutilated	modulated	
interrogate	reinstated	moderate	regulates

1. Seeds _____ and grow into a tall tree.

2. _____ means to shed off imperceptibility.

3. Don't _____ in greeting elderly people

4. _____ in detail to know the truth.

5. It _____ the function.

6. She _____ the sound well.

7. _____ yourself for longer and healthier life.

8. _____ from the services.

9. _____ by will power.

10. _____ to one's original post.

11. The needle _____ smoothly.

12. One cannot _____ a dead soul.

13. Her vision was _____

14. It was just a _____

15. They have _____ from the United Kingdom.

16. The _____ was in our favour.

Choose the correct words from the following table and fill in the blanks to make meaningful phrases.

stab	steal	stand
steel	stiff	spot
stick	song	stop
speaking	stone	sound
stage	southerly	steam
spur	spread	stake
split	square	smart

1. - - - - - some out

2. Warm - - - - - blowing

3. Make a - - - - - and dance

4. On - - - - - terms

5. - - - - - hair

6. A - - - - - chick

7. - - - - - like wildfire

8. On the - - - - - of the moment

9. A - - - - - meal

10. - - - - - someone in the back

11. - - - - - one's claim

12. Suffer from - - - - - fright

13. - - - - - in a good stead

14. - - - - - a march on

15. Full - - - - - ahead

16. Have nerves of - - - - -

17. - - - - - together

18. Leave no - - - - - unturned

19. Keep a - - - - - upper lip

20. - - - - - at nothing

Chapter 4

Comparison

Study the following table carefully. There is a list of comparisons in the form of phrases. Read them aloud and understand their meanings.

Comparisons

As bitter as gall	As bright as silver	As round as a ball
As blind as a bat	As bright as full moon	As sharp as a needle
As brave as a lion	As bright as the sun	As silent as a grave
As brittle as glass	As black as pitch	As smooth as marble
As black as coal	As busy as a bee	As smooth as velvet
As clear as crystal	As cool as cucumber	As soft as silk
As cold as ice	As cunning as a fox	As sour as vinegar
As cheerful as a lark	As deep as a well	As stupid as a donkey
As dry as a bone	As easy as ABC	As sweet as honey
As dumb as a statue	As firm as a rock	As timid as a hare
As fast as a hare	As fair as arose	As white as milk
As fresh as dew	As free as air	As regular as a clock
As fierce as a lion	As grave as a judge	As sharp as a knife
As gentle as a lamb	As good as gold	As sharp as razor
As green as grass	As hard as a stone	As smooth as glass
As greedy as a wolf	As hot as fire	As smooth as butter
As harmless as a dove	As hungry as a wolf	As smooth as oil
As heavy as lead	As innocent as a dove	As soft as wax
As hungry as a hawk	As light as air	As straight as crow-flight
As innocent as a leaf	As meek as a lamb	As sure as death
As loud as thunder	As playful as a squirrel	As swift as an arrow
As obstinate as a mule	As proud as a peacock	As white as snow
As pale as death	As red as blood	As wise as King Solomon
As quick as lightning	As rich as a Jew	

Use as many phrases or Comparisons listed in the table (previous page) in sentences of your own and understand their meanings in a better way.

Collective Nouns

Following is a table of collections in the form of phrases. Read them aloud and understand their meanings. Also try to learn these collective nouns and their usage.

Collective Nouns and their Usage

A ball of string	A joint of meat	A collection of stamps
A bar of chocolate	A loaf of bread	A company of soldiers
A bunch of flowers	A number of coins	A crowd of people
A cake of soap	A pack of cards	A fleet of boats
A flight of stairs	A packet of needles	A fleet of ships
A flight of stairs	A piece of cake	A herd of cows
A flock of birds	A slice of cake	A herd of cattle
A flock of geese	A plate of sandwiches	A herd of deer
A gang of workmen	A roll of paper	A herd of swine
A group of trees	A ream of paper	A volley of shots
A posse of trees	A skin of silk	A lock of hair
A row of houses	A team of players	A board of directors
A heap of stones	A band of singers	A bundle of sticks
A heap of ruins	A band of musicians	A code of laws
A heap of sand	A bevy of ladies	A crate of bottles
A party of tourists	A bevy of girls	A crate of crockery
A pile of blankets	A bevy of merchants	A pair of shoes
A reel of thread	A caravan of travelers	A box of shoes
A stale of stone	A caravan of pilgrims	A set of tools
An army of soldiers	A cluster of stars	A troupe of scouts
A batch of students	A cluster of grapes	A troupe of dancers
A consignment of goods	A course of lectures	A suite of rooms

A choir of singers	A series of lectures	A broach of chickens
A crew of sailors	A basket of fruits	A bundle of hay
A collection of relics	A huddle of beggars	A league of nations
A collection of curiosities	A library of books	A ring of keys
A bundle of books	A set books	A horde of robbers
A dove cattle	A list of articles	A horde prairies
A flight of birds	A series of articles	An anthology of poems
A flight of locusts	A lot of merchandise	A scoop of journalists
A swarm of locusts	A multitude of people	A pack of hounds
A group of islands	A mass of clouds	A stud of horses
A bitter of puppies	A series of rallies	A string of camels
A nest of ants	A nest of rabbits	A tuft of hair
A hill of ants	A pack of wolves	A tuft of grass
A bouquet of flowers	A sheaf of grain	A tribe of natives
A chain of mountains	A sheaf of corn	A brood of chickens/hens
A constellation of stars	A sheaf of arrows	A dule of doves
A mob of people	A quiver of arrows	A stolid of flamingoes
A range of mountains	A flock of birds	A parliament of owls
A range of cliffs	A siege of cranes	A pride of peacocks
A swarm of bees	A flush of dicks	A pod of pelicans
A series of events	A team of geese	A wake of vultures
A volley of questions	A company of parrots	A troop of apes
A shoal of fish	A flight of pigeons	A team of oxen
A stack of wood	A host of sparrows	A grind of whales
A century of years	A herd of antelopes	A cloud of ghosts
A millennium of years	A colony of bats	A bench of judges/bishops
A decade of years	A litter of pups	An orchestra of musicians
A class of students	A colony of ants	A den of thieves
A class of persons	A faculty of academics	A worship of writers
A congress of delegates	A panel of experts	A fleet of cars
A clutch of eggs	A house of senators	A chain of islands
A curriculum of studies	A congregation of worshippers	A string of pearls
A federation of associations	A host of angels	A giggle of girls
A federation of states	A network of computers	A pack of suitcases

Use as many phrases (Collective Nouns) in sentences of your own to excel in speech and improve your vocabulary.

Chapter 6

Singular & Plural Nouns

When a noun is in singular number or just one in number, it is said to be a **Singular Noun**, and when a noun is in plural number or more than one, then it is said to be in **Plural Number**. For example, Man ⇨ Men; Cow ⇨Cows; Aeroplane ⇨ Aeroplanes, etc. However, there are certain nouns, which remain the same in both the singular and plural forms such as: Sheep⇨ Sheep; Deer⇨ Deer; Fish⇨ Fish, etc.

Study the chart below carefully:

List of Singular & Plural Nouns

Singular	Plural	Singular	Plural
alga	⇨ algae	crisis	⇨ crises
alto	⇨ altos	criterion	⇨ criteria
analysis	⇨ analyses	crux	⇨ crux
antithesis	⇨ antitheses	dado	⇨ dadoes
apex	⇨ apexes; apices	datum	⇨ data
appendix	⇨ appendices	dictum	⇨ dicta
appendix	⇨ appendixes (anatomy)	dynamo	⇨ dynamos
aquarium	⇨ aquaria; aquariums	echo	⇨ echoes
archepelago	⇨ archepelagos	elf	⇨ elves
automation	⇨ automata	emporium	⇨ emporia
axe	⇨ axes	enigma	⇨ enigmas
bacillus	⇨ bacilli	erratum	⇨ errata
bacterium	⇨ bacteria	Eskimo	⇨ Eskimos
bamboo	⇨ bamboos	euphonium	⇨ euphoniums
basis	⇨ bases	flamingo	⇨ flamingoes
cactus	⇨ cacti	focus	⇨ focuses
calyx	⇨ calyces	folio	⇨ folios

Singular		Plural	Singular		Plural
cherub	⇨	cherubim; cherubs	formula	⇨	formulas; formulae
concerto	⇨	concertos	forum	⇨	forums
corps	⇨	corps	fresco	⇨	frescoes
corrigendum	⇨	corrigenda	fulcrum	⇨	fulcrums
crematorium	⇨	crematoria	fungus	⇨	fungi
genesis	⇨	geneses	mummy	⇨	mummies
genius	⇨	geniuses	narcissus	⇨	narcissi; narcissuses
genus	⇨	genera	nebula	⇨	nebulae
gladiolus	⇨	gladioli	no	⇨	noes
half	⇨	halves	nucleus	⇨	nuclei
hoof	⇨	hoofs; hooves	oasis	⇨	oases
harmonium	⇨	harmoniums	octopus	⇨	octopuses
hippopotamus	⇨	hippopotamuses; hippopotami	parenthesis	⇨	parentheses
hypothesis	⇨	hypotheses	pendulum	⇨	pendulums
igloo	⇨	igloos	phenomenon	⇨	phenomena
ignoramus	⇨	ignoramuses	plateau	⇨	plateau; plateaux
index	⇨	indexes; indices (math)	poet-laureate	⇨	poets-laureate
innuendo	⇨	innuendos	polyanthus	⇨	polyanthuses
isthmus	⇨	isthmuses	portfolio	⇨	portfolios
kilo	⇨	kilos	premium	⇨	premiums
lacuna	⇨	lacunas; lacunae	prospectus	⇨	prospectuses
larva	⇨	larvae	proviso	⇨	provisos
libretto	⇨	librettos; libretti	quiz	⇨	quizzes
linoleum	⇨	linoleums	quorum	⇨	quorums
maestro	⇨	maestros; maestri	quota	⇨	quotas
matrix	⇨	matrices	rabbi	⇨	rabbies
mausoleum	⇨	mausoleums	radius	⇨	radii
maximum	⇨	maxima	referendum	⇨	referendums
medium	⇨	media; mediums (spiritualism)	rhino	⇨	rhinos
memorandum	⇨	memoranda	rhinoceros	⇨	rhinoceros
menu	⇨	menus	roof	⇨	roofs
minimum	⇨	minima	rostum	⇨	rostrums

Singular		Plural	Singular		Plural
momentum	⇨	momenta; momentum	rota	⇨	rotas
mongoose	⇨	mongeese; mongooses	rotunda	⇨	rotundas
mosquito	⇨	mosquitoes	salmon	⇨	salmon
mother-in-law	⇨	mothers-in-law	sanatorium	⇨	sanatoriums; sanatoria
motto	⇨	mottoes	serf	⇨	serfs
sheriff	⇨	sheriffs	terminus	⇨	terminuses; termini
silo	⇨	silos	thesis	⇨	theses
solarium	⇨	solariums; solaria	tomato	⇨	tomatoes
salo	⇨	salos	torpedo	⇨	torpedoes
species	⇨	species	trauma	⇨	traumata
spectrum	⇨	spectra	tumulus	⇨	tumuli
sphinx	⇨	sphinxes	turf	⇨	turfs
stadium	⇨	stadiums; stadia	two	⇨	twos
stamen	⇨	stamens	ultimatum	⇨	ultimatums
stand-by	⇨	stand-bys	vacuum	⇨	vacuums; vascua
stimulus	⇨	stimuli	vertebra	⇨	vertebrae
stratum	⇨	strata	veto	⇨	vetoes
stylo	⇨	stylos	virtuso	⇨	virtuosi
stylus	⇨	styluses	virus	⇨	viruses
syllabus	⇨	syllabuses; syllabi	vista	⇨	vistas
symposium	⇨	symposia	volcano	⇨	volcanoes
talisman	⇨	talismans	vortex	⇨	vortices
tabaleau	⇨	tabaleaux			

Use most of the nouns in sentences of your own, both in Singular and Plural forms.

Chapter 7

Adjectives

Describing words are called Adjectives. They are called so as they describe or tell something about a noun/pronoun. Following is a table or list of Adjectives with nouns/pronouns. Read them carefully and use them in your daily conversations to enhance your command over the language.

List of Adjectives

loose dress	a veteran thief	low attendance
tight dress	confirmed service	long, long ago
vulgar dress	authentic news	a sensible person
narrow path	vulgar pictures	deeply felt
nasty blow	hasty step	a learned teacher
rough surface	registered document	a powerless politician
steep stair	ripe fruit/time	an elevated door
strong pillar	tight nut	elder son
great beauty	nice weather	dense forest
intense heat	terribly hot	a large house
high fever	ice cold	a secret meeting
lots of things	a great deal of noise	great fear
acute pain	regular fun	running machine
severe pain	enormous profit	dusty path
warm hospitality	warm sympathy	dangerous appearance
huge loss	profound sorrow	deep intimacy
glaring mistake	deeply worried	serious case
gross blunder	fine silk	meaningless talk
silken lining	service spoon	a brick built house
incessant joy	tasty preparation	air tight living
real delight	delightful days	serious injury
high praise	a long way off	living moments
cemented path	bushy field	lifeless living

grave doubt	ambiguous statement	a sensitive moment
fast colour	coarse cloth	great scarcity
a reliable person	skilled work	superfluous statement
precious eyes	slim girl	a powerful figure
deceptive collaboration	obese lady	a sanctioned post
metalled footpath	lean hope	a short cut
sharp turning	faint voice	youngest daughter
worried look	injured body	dark street
weakened organs	sick parents	a closed circuit
sold goods	diligent student	a standard method
timely departure	net gain	real fame
correct guess	reduced rate	rejected abode
sudden loss	grey hair	dilly dally tactics
gross mistake	sweet fruits	severe attack
substantial tax	green/dry leaves	grave doubt
false statement	heavy articles	humorous joke
thick boughs	cultivated land	correct advice
fast friend	multi storeyed building	a little tea
cooked vegetables	pleasant atmosphere	completed deal
sold commodity	urgent matter	dangerous fall
tender age	dead spirit	quick decision
a raw hand	lively ideas	limited period
deviated move	lasting illusion	full done chicken
balanced step	discoloured shirt	airy hut
experienced employee	a few grains	closed cabin
half done meat	blind ally	a straw house
positive proof	indebted person	detailed report
lighted cottage	certified copy	sound advice
slender means	smooth passage	clean pond
scant report	tired body	slippery hold
defective weapon	tested machine	pleasant dream
practical approach	new arrival	doubtful start
fishy idea	delayed start	central location
mature move	surprising defeat	loose motion
a fat figure	calculated income	working mason
early morning	smooth writing	much water
late night movie	intelligent boy	wounded animal
fine fabric	early morning	smooth writing
much water	late night movie	intelligent boy
wounded animal	fine fabric	

EXERCISE

Use these Adjective phrases in sentences of your own to increase your vocabulary.

Chapter 8

Verbs

List of Verbs

For correct or exact use or expression, it is essential to read and learn the usage of the following verbs and phrases as in English, different verbs are used for the expression of different actions.

Cutting	to prepare salad
to clip moustache	to dress a cake
to trim the beard	to cook food
to pare the nails	to serve food
to fell the tree	
to hew out stone	**Court**
to prune the hedge	to pray to court
to slash the marks	to surrender to court
to deduct the salary	to submit papers
to reap crops	to take bail
to waste time	to grant a bail
to kill time	
to cut one's throat	**Give**
to book the ticket	to give; to offer
	to allow; to permit
Cooking	to instruct; to teach
to bake bread	to pay rent; to pay fare
to cook rice	to direct
to boil an egg	to curse
to roast meat	to punish
to fry vegetables	to punish

to prison; to imprison	to congratulate
to jail; to send to jail	to meet the expenses
to advise; to give opinion	to console; to give consolation
to fall; to make fall	to give importance
to pull down	to cheat; to deceive
to pay attention	to paralyse
to make a statement	to dedicate
to apply; to send an application	to humiliate
to submit an application	to separate
to resign	to commit suicide
to reduce; to deduct	to make progress
to employ; to give employment	to refer to
to frighten	to complete a task
to burn a house	to observe fast
to light a lamp	to cultivate the field
to switch on the light	to take up arms
to taunt	to ask for accounts
to set free	to receive salary
to prescribe medicine	to take revenge
to administer medicines	to show respect
to turn out; to expel	to show kindness
to dive away	to make delay
to bribe	to auction articles
to give relief	to imitate others
to provide comfort	to repent for misdeeds
to inject; to administer an injection	to invent ideas
to give alms	to finish questioning
to deliver a lecture	to protest against
to make a speech	to make a promise
to refuse; to decline; to deny	to prompt from behind
winding a watch	to play false
to water; to irrigate	to have/show pride
to deliver a letter	to draw conclusions
to offer food	to cancel programme
to pay the price	to strike off
to run temperature	to sit for an examination
to cut throat	to take an exam
to pretend illness	to appear at an exam
to calculate loss	to inform; to notify
to inflict injury	to run temperature
to dry out	to cut throat

to play tricks
to consult a doctor
to fire a gun
to consult a dictionary
to go on strike
to bring harm
to hold a feast

Do
to throw mud
to box the ear
to punish for mistake
to threat with a case
to file a petition
to draw a case
to defend a case
to lodge a complaint
to plead guilty
to send word
to squander wealth
to abuse
to blame
to give up
to abandon
to introduce
to produce evidence
to be a witness
to look after
to speak ill
to turn down a request
to identify the thief
to make an excuse
to elaborate a point
to implement orders
to dismiss an employee/case
to solve a problem
to reduce; to abbreviate

to combine; to unite
to uproot; to root out
to pull off
to give a word
to set a price
to serve the dish
to fill up
to take away
to receive charity
to win the heart
to invite trouble
to feel the pulse
to find out; to enquire into
to levy a fine
to realise a fine
to take an oath
to take permission
to take to task
to charge rent/fee/fare
to obtain consent
to produce an effect
to speed up
to confess a crime
to accept mistakes
to multiply medals
to settle a dispute
to give birth to
to have breakfast
to lock up
to touch shore
to create a scene
to take root
to cast an evil eye
to pick one's pocket
to hold a meeting
to organize a match

English Vocabulary made Easy

Chapter 9

Miscellaneous

An adverb, as we know is a word that can be added to a verb to modify its meaning. Basically, an adverb tells you when, where, how, in what manner or to what extent an action is performed. Following is a list of Adverbs and **Conjunctions** that can be used in day to day life conversations in English. You can learn them and frame sentences with as many of them as possible to enhance and improve your vocabulary.

Conjunctions on the other hand, are words that join two or more words, phrases or clauses to make a sentence. e.g., (1) Ram **and** Raghu are childhood friends. (2) He fell down **suddenly** from the bus. In these two examples **'and'** is a Conjunction; **'suddenly'** is an Adverb.

Adverbs and Conjunctions

suddenly	clearly	though
all of a sudden	widely	the whole
so	otherwise	everywhere
therefore	at times	wherever
by turns	till	generally
when	a little	ordinarily
sometime or the other	clearly	really
whenever	widely	actually
anyone	otherwise	by the way
as	at times	despite
so that	till	so much so that
more or less	a little	by chance
day by day	in broad day light	slowly
but	again	wildly
again and again	chiefly	once upon a time
in spite of	here and there	occasionally
always	although	slight

Cries of Birds

apes	⇨	gibber	horses	⇨	neigh
monkeys	⇨	chatter	jackals	⇨	howl
asses	⇨	bray	kites	⇨	scream
bears	⇨	growl	lambs	⇨	bleat
bees	⇨	hum	lions	⇨	roar
birds	⇨	chirp	mice	⇨	squeak
bulls	⇨	bellow	nightingales	⇨	sing
calves	⇨	bleat	owl	⇨	hoot
camels	⇨	grunt	oxen	⇨	low
cats	⇨	mew	parrots	⇨	chatter
cattle	⇨	low	parrots	⇨	talk
cocks	⇨	crow	pigs	⇨	grunt
cows	⇨	low	pigeons	⇨	coo
dogs	⇨	bark	puppies	⇨	yelp
doves	⇨	coo	ravens	⇨	creak
ducks	⇨	quack	snakes	⇨	hiss
elephants	⇨	trumpet	sheep	⇨	bleat
flies	⇨	buzz	swans	⇨	cry
foxes	⇨	bark	tigers	⇨	growl
geese	⇨	cackle	turkeys	⇨	gobble
frogs	⇨	croak	vultures	⇨	scream
goats	⇨	bleat	wolves	⇨	howl
howls	⇨	scream	wolves	⇨	growl
hens	⇨	cluck			

Sounds of Objects

bells	⇨	ring	guns	⇨	boom
boots	⇨	creak	steam	⇨	hiss
bugles	⇨	blow	teeth	⇨	chatter
coins	⇨	jingle	streams	⇨	bubble
clocks	⇨	tick	trains	⇨	rumble
clouds	⇨	thunder	wheels	⇨	rattle
dishes	⇨	rattle	hinges	⇨	creak

fire	⇨	crackles	hands	⇨	clap
hoofs	⇨	clatter	weapons	⇨	clatter
leaves	⇨	rustle	wind	⇨	howl
rain	⇨	patter	wind	⇨	whistle
engines	⇨	whistle	wing	⇨	flap
metal	⇨	rings	feet	⇨	patter
shoes	⇨	creak	aeroplane	⇨	zoom

Terms from the Business World

Account book	Accountant	Accounting Year
Assessment	Assessment Year	Access
Accrued Interest	Active Capital	After Date Hundy
Allowances	Annual Return	Annual Stock Checking
Annual Report	Annual Net Profit	Arrears
Average	Banking	Banker
Bank account	Bank Balance	Balance
Bad debts	Bank Charge	Bank Interest
Bankrupt	Bankruptcy	Bill
Bill book	Bill Journal	Bill for collection
Bill for payment	Black Market	Black Money
Bill for sale	Bill Received	Blank Book
Borrow	Bonus	Bribe
Billion exchange	Billion Market	Bottom Price
Capital	Capital Interest	Capital Value
Cash	Cash Book	Cash Scroll
Cashier	Charges	Chartered Accountant
Cash payment	Cash Flow	Cash Deposit
Clean Bill	Clean Chit	Conversion
Conversion Table	Cost	Cost Account
Cost Accountant	Cash Register	Credit
Credit Book	Credit Note	Current Account
Currency	Current Trend	Current Deposit
Customer	Customer Service	Customer Centre
Customer's account	Customer's flow	Debt

Debtors	Deflation	Demand
Demand Note	Demand Loan	Deposit
Deposit Register	Deposit Ledger	Deposit voucher
Depreciation	Discharged Loan	Discount
Dishonoured Checque	Due Date	Earning
Earn leave	Employee	Employer
Employment	Exchange rate	Export
Export duty	Excess billing	Extra Discount
Extra Payment	Exchequer	Finance
Financer	Financial	Fixed asset
Fixed Deposit	Floatation	Foreign Exchange
Free market	Free Of Charge	Freight
File	Goods	Godown
Gate Pass	Hard Currency	Hoarding
Hush Money	House	Home Delivery
House Rent	Hard times	Hand in hand
In Hand	In Transit	Investment
Interest	Interest rate	Industrialist
Industry	Industrial	Intervention
Job	Judgment	Jealous
Lend	Letter	Letterhead
Letter of consent	Letter of Credit	Loan
Loan Balance	Local Cheque	Lost in Transit
Labour	Labour Problem	Law
Labour Law	Litigation	Legal Action
Legal View	Legal Opinion	Livelihood
Line	Mark	Make
Maker's Brand	Market	Market Survey
Money	Monetary Gain	Monetary Value
Marketability	Money Market	Net income
Net Sale	Net Income	Net Profit
Office	Office Set	Official
Official Paper	Opening Balance	Order Cheque
Open Delivery	Outside	Outstanding
Paper	Paper Chip	Paper Clip

Partner	Partnership	Partnership Agreement
Pay	Pay Slip	Payment
Payee	Price	Price List
Price Check	Pre Paid	Preparation
Public Money	Public Credit	Project
Project Report	Public Issue	Pursuit
Performance	Profit	Professional
Realisation	Reimbursement	Remind
Reminder	Recall	Receipt Book
Running Cash	Running Credit	Sale
Sold Goods	Salesmen	Sales Register
Saving Bank	Saving Account	Soft Currency
Stock	Stock Exchange	Stockist
Stock Transfer	Tight Money	Trading Capital
Time Deposit	Trade	Tradesmen
Trend	Utility	Withdrawal
Undertaking	Work	Worker
Work Order	Working Hour	Vocation

Words Related to Battle

War	Warfare	Hostilities
Bloodshed	Fighting	Clash
Conflict	Combat	Weapons
Arms	Armament	Arsenal
Armour	Arrow	Quarrel
Dart	Shaft	Bow
Bolt	Wire	Arbalest
Long Bow	Cross Bow	Firearms
Sling	Ballista	Cannon
Artillery	Battery	Ordnance
Gun	Gunnery	Muzzle Loader
Rifle	Carbine	Machine Gun
Shot Gun	Automatic	Revolver
Bazooka	Pistol	Missile
Derringer	Antiaircraft	

Projectile	Trajectile	Bullet
Slug	Shot	Pellet
Cannon Ball	Shrapnel	Grenade
Shell	Bomb	Block Buster
Robot	Bomb	Napalm Bomb
Atom Bomb	Hydrogen Bomb	A-Bomb
Gas Bomb	Depth Bomb	Ammunition
Explosive	Cartridge	Powder
Gun Powder	Dynamite	Submarine
Tnt	Poison Gas	Wmd
Lewisite	Chlorine Gas	Gas Mask
Brute Force	Magazine	Chemical Weapons
Auxiliary Force	Mutiny	Navy
Defence	Trench	Aggression
Cease Fire	Army Troops	Cold War
Infantry	Fortification	Treaty
Cavalry	Recruitment	Bombardment
Battleship	Strategy	Operation
Commander	Blockade	Siege

Common Words from Sanskrit

Achitti	ignorance; unconsciousness
Adhik ra	capacity; the immediate power that determines right
Adhyaksha	presiding person
Adhy ropa	imposition
Advaita	Monism
Agni	Fire; Fire God
Ahank ra	ego; ego-idea
Akshar	immutable; that which can't be cut; immobile
nanda	bliss; delight; beatitude
Anirvachaniya	inexpressible; inexplicable; ineffable
Anumant	the giver of the sanction
Apar rdha	the lower hemisphere; lower half
Asat	non-being; the negation of all existence
Asura	devil; adversary of the gods

Ashwattha	Banyan tree; symbol of the cosmic manifestation
tm	self; soul; spirit
tmashakti	self-power; soul power; spiritual power
Avidy	ignorance
Bhakta	a devotee of the God; devotee of the Divine
Bhay nak	terrible
Bibhatsa	horrible; repellent
Brahmaloka	the world of the Brahma
Brahma	The Absolute God
Brahm	God among Indian Trinity; the Creator
Brahma-vidy	the science of knowing the Brahma
Brihat	vast; wide; large
Chaitya Purush	psychic entity; individual soul
Chitta	pure consciousness
Chitti	knowledge
Deva	god; Godhead
Dharma	law; standard of truth; law of action; (religion)
Hath-yogi	One who practices extreme yoga
Hridaya	heart
Ishwar	God; the Divine Entity; the Absolute God
Jada-vat	like an inert thing
Jiv tm	individual soul
Jugups	shrinking; contraction; self-protecting; recoil
K li	the Primordial Energy; the Divine Power; Creator Mother; the Universal *Mother*
Karma	action; work
Karuna	sorrowful
Karun	compassion;
Kshar	mobile or mutable
Leel	play; game; illusory playfulness; manipulation;
M nas	mind; the sense mind
Manomaya	the mental being; soul in a being
Sachchid nand	sat = existence; chitt =consciousness; nand =bliss; the Absolute Form of the three; the Divine Being
S drishya	likeness
Saguna	the Eternal with infinite qualities

Shakti	energy; force; will power; soul force; the Primordial Goddess of Energy
Sam dhi	inner trance; meditation in trance; Yoga trance;
S nkhya	a system of philosophy; one of the six most primitive Indian philosophy; spiriitual practice
Sany si	an ascetic; one who renounces the world
Shiva	the First Purush who divided Himself into Male and Female; One of the Gods of Eternal Trinity; the Destroyer
Soma	the sacred energetic drink
Shruti	hearing; inspired revelation; out of two one section of Vedic Scriptures
Shunya	void; nothingness; nihil
Sushupti	deep sleep
Svabh va	principle of the Self becoming Nature; the essential nature
Swadharma	own law of action; personal righteous principles
Swarupa	self form
Tamas	the principle of inertia; the darkness; the force of in-conscience; ignorance
T masik	governed by the principle of obscurity and inertia; one of the three qualities
Tapa	literally 'heat'; the act of imbibing Divine Force; principle of energy
Tapasy	effort; act of absorbing cosmic energy; austerity of personal will;
V yu	air; the God of Air; wind; breath; life in a body; the God of life
Veda	endless collection of Eternal Scriptures; all knowledge; books of knowledge
Ved nta	Brahma-Sutra: a book that concludes all discussion about Brahma; one of the six Primordial Indian Philosophies
Vidy	knowledge: Goddess of Knowledge and Creation
Vishnu	one of the Gods of Indian Trinity; the Sustainer; Fosterer
Vishwa-M nava	the Universal Man; the concept that all human beings have born out of one parents
Yoga	union; the final Union of the Soul with the Brahma; one of the six Eternal Indian Philosophies

Compound Words

news stand	anteroom	shake hand
flowerpot	flower petal	pigtail
sand paper	sand watch	sand dune
thunderbolt	thumb talk	copper wire
silver paint	eye colour	bedrock

bedshore	bedsheet	handbag
hand woven	paper pin	paper clip
bud pot	finger purse	snow storm
head crayon	brow bit	brow lid
eyelash	eyelid	eye glass
time pill	antisocial	biochemistry
coordinate	extraordinary	infrastructure
interrelated	interconnected	intramural
neo-romantic	metaphysical	mid town
mid-term	life like	minim bike
self service	overanxious	non-violent
supermarket	signboard	single handed
underhand	half sister	half-brother
stock broker	stock exchange	stock market
state level	homesick	heavenward
playground	looking glass	firefly
softball	childlike	redhead
keyboard	makeup	notebook
mass production	mass communication	real estate
middle finger	middle class	full moon
moonlight	half sister	step brother
step mother	attorney general	part time
full pay	half said	high rate
headgear	cabinet rank	passers by
court martial	coeditor	co-education

Words used in Pairs

alpha and omega	ancient and modern	horse and cart
bag and baggage	bright or dark	hill and dale
bow and arrow	bread and butter	house and home
bread and milk	bound hand and foot	kith and kin
cocks and crows	fire and sword	knife and fork
flesh and blood	fire and light	night and day
flood and wind	heaven and earth	nail and hammer
high and low	head and tail	pins and needles

pipe and tobacco
profit and loss
peace and pleasure
root and branch
son and daughter
sin and misery
sheep and goat
seed and field
science and art
sale and profit
tea and coffee
town and country
taste and spice
wise and foolish
wife and children
bright or dark
holy and happy
drunk or sober
by hook or crook
fair and square
the long and short
rough and ready
null and void
rich or poor
slow and steady
rank and file
first and foremost
likes and dislikes
heart and soul
hue and cry
stuff and nonsense

loaves and fishes
paper and ink
power and pleasure
rack and ruin
skin and bone
sleep and death
soul and body
singer and writer
sale and purchase
tooth and nail
time and tide
truck and trolley
wind and weather
wear and tear
for better or worse
dead and gone
fair or foul
hole and corner
ebb and flow
free and easy
slow and sure
more or less
right and left
kind and true
war and peace
great and small
law and order
give and take
hard and fast
husband and wife
man and beast

now or never
past and present
light and shade
shed and shadow
part and parcel
pros and cons
sum and substance
ups and downs
stark and stiff
odds and ends
ways and means
such and such
round and round
puff and blow
beck and call
fits and starts
humming and hawing
old and grey
cap and tie
uses and abuses
length and breadth
time and again
so and so
push and pull
again and again
by and by
give and take
lock and key
over and above

English Vocabulary made Easy

Chapter 10

Double Letters

In English, there are numerous words that contain double letters: both vowels and consonants. Even the common and popular words among them pose problems. Some double consonants are written habitually, hence, automatically, they come to you, while others present difficulties. It is always advisable to look at them carefully and in a systematic order to win over the ensuing difficulties. Many examples are not needed so, examples with only letters, B and C have been given with many exercises to show the way the words grow.

Words that contain ~bb~

abbacy	abbe	abbey
abbot	abbess	abbreviate
babble	babbitt	bobbin
bubble	bobbery	bobbish
bobby	cabbage	cabbala
cabbie	dabble	dribble
cobble	chubby	ebb
flabby	gibbon	gobble
gabble	gobbet	hobble
hobby	jabber	nibble
pebble	rabbi	rabbit
rabble	ribbon	robber
rubbet	rubbit	rubber
rubbish	rubble	Sabbath
sribble	shabby	squabble
stubble	stubborn	tabby
tebbad	wobble	

EXERCISES

Make sentences with the following words which have not been included in the given list in the previous page.

dribbling	grabbing	hobnobbing
nabbed	nebbish	obbligato
clobber	lubbard	stabbing

Mark carefully how the words grow, and try to understand and learn them.

hobble	hobbler	hobblingly
hobble-bush	hobble-skirt	hobbledeboy
hobbled-boydom	hobbled-boyhood	hobbled-boyism
hobbled-boyish		

Words with ~cc~

accede	accelerate	accent
accept	access	accident
accommodate	accord	accompany
accomplish	accord	accost
account	accrue	accustom
accurate	accurse	accuse
broccoli	coccyx	eccentric
ecclesiastic	eccrinology	impeccable
hiccup	moccasin	piccolo
occasion	occult	occur
soccer	succeed	succor
succubus	tobacco	vaccinate

Make sentences with the following words which have not been included in the above list.

succession	succulent	vaccine
broccoli	raccoon	accentuate
laccolite	accomplice	accomplishment

Mark carefully how the words grow, and make sure you understand and learn them.

access	accessory	accessibility
accessible	accessibly	accession
accessory	accessorial	accessorily

Fill up and complete the words with double letters.

Sp ~ ~ d	H ~ ~ or	Fl ~ ~ t	Co ~ ~ idor
Su ~ ~ umb	Devot ~ ~	Gl ~ ~ m	Co ~ ~ ent
Ca ~ ~ r	Scr ~ ~ n	Ch ~ ~ r	Smi ~ ~ en
Proc ~ ~ d	Sta ~ ~	Sy ~ ~ able	A ~ ~ roval
Stre ~ ~	Est ~ ~ m	Sli ~ ~ ery	Du ~ ~ y
So ~ ~ er	Ante ~ ~ a	Co ~ ~ and	Che ~ ~ y
Sm ~ ~ th	Vac ~ ~ m	Scro ~ ~	Cr ~ ~ per
Expre ~ ~	Handcu ~ ~	Sni ~ ~	Co ~ ~ iery
F ~ ~ ble	Co ~ ~ ect	Cri ~ ~ led	Plat ~ ~ n
Pa ~ ~ ion	Co ~ ~ une		

Fill up and complete the words with double letters.

A ~ ~ ract	A ~ ~ ect	Bl ~ ~ d	Comi ~ ~ ion
A ~ ~ emble	A ~ ~ urance	Co ~ ~ odity	Counse ~ ~ or
A ~ ~ irm	A ~ ~ laim	Di ~ ~ erent	Distre ~ ~
A ~ ~ uage	A ~ ~ est	Dismi ~ ~ al	Dile ~ ~ a
A ~ ~ itional	Agre ~ ~ ion	Exa ~ ~ gerate	Exce ~ ~ ive
Ba ~ ~ el	Ba ~ ~ et	F la ~ ~ ery	Fu ~ ~ oe
Bla ~ ~ er	Ba ~ ~ le	Fo ~ ~ ower	Fo ~ ~ iage
Ba ~ ~ ery	Ble ~ ~		

Fill up and complete the words with double letters.

Gi ~ ~ ick	Gli ~ ~ er	Swe ~ ~	Su ~ ~ ender
Infla ~ ~ able	Impre ~ ~ ion	Tu ~ ~ le	Te ~ ~ific
I ~ ~ ustrte	I ~ ~ uminate	T ~ ~ ls	To ~ ~ ee
Mu ~ ~ le	Mi ~ ~ ion	Co ~ ~ ection	Co ~ ~ entary
Pa ~ ~ able	Pa ~ ~ age	Ke ~ ~ el	Co ~ ~ ect
Shu ~ ~ le	Stru ~ ~ le	Co ~ ~ idor	Ch ~ ~ r
Scu ~ ~ le	Shi ~ ~ er	Ca ~ ~ iage	Car ~ ~ r
Sli ~ ~ er	Sha ~ ~ ow		

Chapter 11

Silent Letters

There are a large number of words in English in which one or more than one letters are silent. They are not pronounced. They, every often affect the pronunciation. Particularly in India, where people are trained to pronounce half-letters and quarter-letters, or to articulate half sound or quarter sound because of rigorous training in *Devanagari* script and sanskrit words or *tatsam, tadbhava* words. Under this influence, they pronounce even silent letters, very often. Though the last, 'r', at the end of a word is not pronounced, but Indians do pronounce it. It is because of the thickness of lips and tongues also.

Here are examples of some silent letters.

Silent last or middle 'b'

bomb	climb	comb	crumb
debt	doubt	dumb	jamb
lamb	limb	numb	plumb
plumber	subtle	thumb	succumb
tomb	womb	debtor	indebted

Silent middle 'd'

handkerchief	handsome	grandchild	handful
handcuff	sandbag	sandpaper	sandwich
sandstorm	adjacent	adjective	adjoin
adjudge	Wednesday	adjunct	adjure

Silent first and middle 'g'

align	alignment	assignment	campaign
champagne	deign	design	feign
foreigner	gnarled	gnash	gnat
gnaw	gnome	gnu	malign
maligner	benign	reign	resign

| sign | sovereign | consign | consignment |
| assign assignment | signing signed | | |

Silent 'h'

rhetoric	rheumatism	rhinoceros	rhyme
rhythm	catarrh	Rhine	Rhodesia
exhaust	exhibit	exhibition	exhilarate
exhort	forehead	exhibit	exhibition
shepherd	silhouette	Durham	heir

Silent 'l'

balm	calm	calmness	embalm
palm	psalm	qualm	salmon
walk	chalk	talk	yolk
folk	half	calf	calves
Faukner	almond	alms	

Silent 'n'

| autumn | column | condemn | damn |
| hymn | solemn | forlorn | |

Silent 'p'

pneumatic	pneumonia	psalm	psychology
psychic	psychiatrist	psalter	pseudo
pshaw	receipt	psychosis	Ptolemy
ptarmigam	ptisan	coup	Campbell
corps	cupboard	raspberry	attempt
empty	exempt	prompt	consumption
redemption	assumption	temptation	

Silent 'r'

answer	cancer	chancellor	flower
army	card	chart	hard
part			

Silent 's'

apropos	island	aisle	précis
chassis	corps	islet	viscount
debris	demesne		

Silent 't'

batch	butcher	catch	clutch
ditch	etch	hatch	hatchet
ketchup	hutch	itch	ketch
hitch	kitchen	latch	match
notch	patch	pitch	satchel
scratch	snatch	sketch	stitch
stretch	switch	thatch	twitch
watch	witch	wretch	wrestle
hasten	fasten	listen	apostle
bustle	castle	epistle	whistle
often	often	ballet	buffet
cabaret	cachet	crochet	bouquet
croquet	argot	depot	mortgage

Silent 'w'

wrangle	wrap	wreath	wreck
wren	wretch	wriggle	wrinkle
write	wrong	wraith	wreak
wrestle	wrought	wry	wrier
wryly			

SECTION-2
BUILDING VOCABULARY

Chapter 12

Prefixes

A Prefix word placed at the beginning of a word to modify or change its meaning. Prefixes can be classified on the basis of their meanings in the following divisions though, some of them have more than one meaning.

Prefixes which refer to the parts of human body or its functions:

Prefixes	Meanings	Examples
Audi~	hear	audition; auditorium
Cardi~	heart	cardiology; cardiac
Derm~	skin	dermatitis; dermatologist
Hemo~	blood	hemoglobin; hemorrhage
Neph~	kidney	nephritis; nephrology
Neuro~	nerve	neurology; neurosis
Osteo~	bone	osteology; osteopath
Physi~	body	physiology; physiognomy
Psych~	mind	psychology; psychosis
Bio~	life	biology; biography

Prefixes which refer to the environment:

Prefixes	Meanings	Examples
Astro~	star	astronaut; astronomy
Cosmo~	universe	cosmology; cosmonaut
Geo~	earth	geography; geology
Hydro~	water	hydrophobia; hydrology
Aqua~	water	aquarium; aquatic
Photo~	light	photograph; photogenic
Aero~	air	aeronautics; aeroplane
Prefixes	**Meanings**	**Examples**

Pneum~	air	pneumonia; pneumatic
Phono~	sound	phonetic; phonograph
Circum~	around	circumference; circumspect
Socio~	society	sociology; socio-economic
Thermo~	heat	thermoflask; thermometer
Zoo~	animal	zoology; zoologist

Prefixes that denote time:

Ante~	before	antenatal; ante-nuptial
Chrono~	time	chronology; chronometer
Ex~	former	ex-president; ex-principal
Neo~	new	neolothic; neophyte
Paleo~	old	paleolithic; paleography
Pre~	before	precursor; premarital
Post~	after	postdated; postgraduate
Proto~	first	protozoa; protagonist
Re~	again	reconstruct; reorganise
Retro~	backward	retrograde; retroactive

Prefixes which denote numbers:

Ambi~	two	ambiguous; ambivert
Bi~	two	biannual; bilingual
Di~	two	dissect; dioxide
Tri~	three	triplicate; trimester
Quadri~	four	quadruple; quadrilateral
Tetra~	four	tetrameter; tetra-chlorine
Penta~	five	pentagon; pentameter
Mono~	one	monotony; monogamy
Multi~	many	multiple; multi-storeyed
Poly~	many	polygamy; polyclinic
Uni~	one	unicorn; uniform

Prefixes which denote places:

Inter~	between	international; intercontinental
Intra~	inside	intramuscular; intravenous
Pan~	all over	Pan-American; Pan Indian
Prefixes	**Meanings**	**Examples**

Super~	above	superimpose; superscript
Tele~	distance	telephone; telepathy
Out~	distance	outdoor; outpost
Under~	beneath	underwater; undercurrent
Sub~	below	subconscious; suborbital
Tra~	across	transform; traverse
Trans~	through	transform; translate

Prefixes which denote sizes:

Hyper~	extreme	hyperactive; hypertension
Micro~	small	microeconomics; microbiology
Mini~	small	miniature; miniskirt
Ultra~	beyond	ultraviolet; ultrasound
Under~	less	underdeveloped; underestimate

Prefixes which denote positions:

Anti~	against	antisocial; anticlockwise
Counter~	against	counteract; counterattack
Pro~	in favour of	pro-India; pro Germany
Be~	by, near	below; beside
Cata~	downward	cataclysm; catacomb
Com~	with, together	command; company
De~	from, away	depart; descend

Prefixes which show praise or dislike:

Mal~	bad	malnutrition; malfunction
Mis~	wrong	misfortune; misconduct
Pseudo~	false	pseudo-cultural; pseudo-religious
Super~	far better	superman; super-approach
Ultra~	excessively	ultramodern; ultra-rigid

Prefixes which show opposite meanings:

De~	do the opposite of	decentralise; denationalise
Dis~	do the opposite of	disconnect; discolour
Un~	do the opposite of	undo; unpack
Il~	do the opposite of	illegal; illogical

Prefixes which give a negative sense:

A~	not	amoral; a-scientific
Im~	not	imperfect; immaterial
In~	not	inadvertent; inalienable
Ir~	not	irregular; irrelevant
Non~	not	nonviable; non-profitable
Un~	not	unable; unkind

Prefixes which have not been classified:

Ana~	up, through	analysis; anatomy
Ant~	against	antagonist; antacid
Contra~	against	contradict; contrary
Cyclo~	circle	cyclone; cyclopaedia
Dis~	apart	discharge; distract
Dis~	negative	disbelief; discontent
Hetero~	other	heterodox; heterogeneous
Mega~	big	megaphone; mega-mania
Meta~	after, beyond	metaphor; metaphysics
Macro~	long, large	macron; macrocosm
Ob~	in the way	obstruct; obstacle
Olig~	beyond	oligarchy; oligopoly
Out~	beyond	outcast; outburst
Para~	beyond	parable; parallel
Path~	suffering	pathology; pathetic
Per~	throughout	perfect; perform
Retro~	backward	retrograde; retroactive
Sub~	under, inferior	submit; subordinate

Words with the prefix, Dis~ which has a negative meaning:

disable	discontent	disabuse	discontinue
disadvantage	discourage	disaffect	discourteous
disagree	discredit	disallow	disembody
disappear	disenchant	disappoint	distorted
disapprove	distract	disarm	distraction
disarrangement	disarrange	distrust	disturb
disarray	disunion	disassemble	disuse

disaster	disseminate	disband	disserve
disbar	discard	disbelieve	dissociate
disburse	dissolve	discharge	distaste
disclose	disqualify	discolour	disregard
discomfort	disrespect	discompose	disrobe
disconnect	disturb	disturbance	disrupt

Words with the prefix, Mis~ which means wrong or wrongly:

misadvise	misconstrue	misguide	misrepresentation
misadventure	mischief	mishandle	mispronounce
misapply	mischievous	misinform	misinterpret
misalliance	misfortune	mislead	mistreat
misbehave	misfortunate	misplace	mistrial
miscalculate	mishap	misquote	mistrust
miscarriage	mishap	misspell	misconstrue
mischance	misdeed	misstate	mislay
misconceive	misogamy	misplacement	misconduct
misgovern	misconstrue	misprint	miscreant
misdeal	misfire	mismanage	mistake

Words with the prefix, In~ which gives a negative meaning:

inability	inauspicious	indefatigable	indiscriminate
inaccessible	incalculable	indefinite	indispensible
inaccurate	incapable	indellible	ineducable
inaction	incompatible	indelicate	ineffable
inactive	incompetent	indemnify	ineffective
inadequate	incomprehensible	independence	ineligible
inadmissible	inconceivable	indestructible	inequality
inanimate	inconclusive	indeterminate	inescapable
inappropriate	inconsequential	indifferent	inexhaustible
inarticulate	incurable	indigestible	inexpressible
inattentive	indecision	indirect	inextinguishable
infallible	infamous	inflexible	inglorious

Words with the prefix, Im~ which means 'not' and is used in a negative sense.

It is usually applied before the words beginning with three letters: b; m and p.

imbalance	immoderate	impalpable	impede
imbecile	immodest	impanel	impediment
imbed	immoral	impart	impel
imbroglio	immortal	impartial	impend
imbue	immovable	impasse	impenetrable
immaterial	immune	impassible	impenitent
immature	immunity	impassion	imperative
immeasurable	immunise	impassive	imperceptible
immediacy	immure	impatient	imperfect
immediate	immutable	impeach	imperil
immemorial	impact	impeccable	imperious
immobile	impair	impecunious	imperishable
impregnate	impale	impinge	impermanent
improbable	impost	impious	impermeable
improper	impostor	implacable	impersonal
impropriety	imposture	implant	impersonate
imprudent	impotent	implausible	impertinent
impurity	impound	impolite	imperturbable
impure	impoverish	imponderable	impetus
impeach	impractical	import	impiety

Words with the prefix, Self~ :

self-abasement	self-confessed	self-discipline	self-imposed
self-accusation	self-confidence	self-distrust	self-improvement
self-acting	self-confident	self-doubt	self-incrimination
self-addressed	self-congratulation	self-educated	self-incriminating
self-administer	self-contradiction	self-employed	self-induced
self-advancement	self-contradicting	self-employment	self-indulgence
self-aggrandizement	self-control	self-esteem	self-inflicted
self-aggrandizing	self-correcting	self-evident	self-interest
self-analysis	self-criticism	self-examination	self-limiting
self-appointed	self-cultivation	self-explaining	self-love
self-asserting	self-deceit	self-explanation	self-lubricating
self-assertion	self-deceiving	self-expression	self-luminous

self-assurance	self-deception	self-forgetful	self-mastery
self-assured	self-defeating	self-fulfilling	self-centred
self-awareness	self-defense	self-giving	self-operating
self-betrayal	self-delusion	self-governing	self-perception
self-closing	self-denial	self-help	self-perpetuating
self-command	self-denying	self-hypnosis	self-pity
self-complacent	self-depreciation	self-identity	self-portrait
self-conceited	self-despair	self-image	self-possessed
self-concern	self-destruction	self-importance	self-possession
self-condemned	self-determination	self-important	self-preservation
self-proclaimed	self-reliance	self-satisfaction	self-sufficient
self-propelled	self-reliant	self-satisfied	self-supporting
self-propelling	self-reproach	self-seeking	self-taught
self-protection	self-respect	self-service	self-torment
self-realisation	self-respecting	self-starting	self-winding
self-regard	self-rule	self-styled	self-worth
self-registering	self-sacrifice	self-sufficiency	self-seeker

Words with the prefix, Sub~ which means under, beneath, or subordinate, etc:

sub-acute	sub-agony	sub-agent	sub-aqueous
sub-arctic	sub-freezing	sub-paragraph	sub-teen
sub-area	sub-genus	sub-parable	sub-temperate
sub-atmospheric	sub-group	sub-phylum	sub-threshold
sub-average	sub-head	sub-plot	sub-topic
sub-basement	sub-heading	sub-polar	sub-treasury
sub-category	sub-human	sub-principal	sub-clause
sub-class	sub-index	sub-problem	sub-type
sub-clinical	sub-interval	sub-professional	sub-unit
sub-contract	sub-kingdom	sub-program	sub-variety
sub-contractor	sub-lease	sub-region	sub-visible
sub- culture	sub-lethal	sub-routine	sub-vocal
sub-deacon	sub-literate	sub-saturated	sub-zero
sub-dean	sub-minimal	sub-section	sub-standard
sub-discipline	sub-minimum	sub-sense	sub-quality
sub-entry	sub-optional	sub-stage	sub-topic

| sub-family | sub-order | sub-system | sub-test |

Words with the prefix, Over~ .

It means so as to exceed or surpass; excessive; excessively.

overeat	overabundance	overabundant	overaggressive
over-oppressive	overambitious	overanxious	overbid
overbold	overbuild	overburden	overbuy
overcapacity	overcapitalise	over-careful	overcautious
overcompensation	overestimate	overindulgence	over-praise
overconfidence	overexcite	overindulgent	overprice
overconfident	overexert	overlarge	overproduce
overcook	overexertion	over-learn	overproduction
overcritical	overextend	over-liberal	overprotect
overcrowd	over-fatigued	overload	over-proud
over-decorated	overfeed	overlong	overrate
overdevelop	over-feel	overmodest	overreact
overdose	overgenerous	overnice	over-refinement
overdress	overgraze	over-optimism	overrepresented
overeager	overhasty	over-optimistic	overripe
overemphasis	overheat	overpay	oversensitive
overenthusiastic	overindulge	overpopulated	oversimplify
overspecialise	overstock	oversupply	overuse
overspend	over-strict	overtax	overvalue

Words with the prefix, Out~ :

out bed	outermost	outlive	outset
out board	outface	outlook	outshine
out bound	outfield	outmoded	outside
outbreak	outfit	out model	outsider
out building	outflank	outnumber	outskirts
outburst	outgo	outpost	outsmart
outcome	outgrowth	outrage	outspoken
outcry	outing	outrange	outstanding
outdated	outlaw	outrank	outstrip
outdo	outlay	outright	outward

| outdoor | outlet | outrun | outweigh |
| outer | outline | outsell | outwit |

Words with the prefix, De~ :

debar	decry	defrost	depopulate
debark	deduct	degenerate	depreciate
decelerate	deface	dehydrate	depress
decipher	defame	deliberate	derail
disclaim	defile	delimit	derange
declassify	deflate	demobilise	descend
declension	deflect	demoralise	de-segregate
declination	deflower	demote	despoil
decline	defoliate	demurrage	dethrone
decode	deforest	denaturalize	detour
décolletage	deform	denature	detract
decompose	deformity	denominate	detraction
decoy	defraud	denude	devaluate
decrease	defray	denunciate	devoid

Words with the prefix, Cat~ :

cataclysm	catamount	catkin	cattail
catacomb	cataract	catmint	catty
catafalque	catbird	catnap	cattier
catalepsy	catboat	catnip	cattiest
catalyses	catcall	cat o' nine tails	cattily
catalyst	catfish	catskill	cattiness
catalyze	cation	cat's paw	catty cornered
catamaran	catgut	catsup	catwalk

Words with the prefix, Hypo~ which means excessive:

hypochondria	hypodermic	hypotenuse	hypothetical
hypochondrias	hyposensitive	hypothecate	hypoxemia
hypocrisy	hypotension	hypothesis	hypoxia

Words with the prefix, Quad~ which means four:

quadrangle	quadric lateral
quadrant	quadrille
quadraphonic	quadruped

quadrate	quadruplet
quadratic	quadruplicate

Words with the prefix, Ill~ which gives a negative sense:

ill advise	ill gotten
ill bred	illiberal
illegal	illimitable
illegible	illiterate
illegitimate	illogical
ill fated	ill starred
ill favoured	ill tempered
ill mannered	ill timed/

EXERCISES

Separate the words given below and prepare two lists:

1. Words with Prefix and

2. Words without Prefix

Chromo	Chromosome	Chronic	Chronicle
Chronological	Chronology	Chromo-meter	Chutney
Cinema	Cinematic	Circle	Circular
Circulation	Circulate	Circumference	Circumflex
Circumfused	Circumlocution	Circumspect	Circumstance
Classic	Classicism	Classified	Classify
Classmate	Classroom	Cocoa	Cocoon
Coeducation	Coefficient	Coequal	Coerce
Coexist	Coffee	Cognate	Cohesion
Collaborate	Collateral	Collect	Collusion

Separate the prefixes from the words given below:

Command	Commandment	Commandant	Cooperate
Concede	Concern	Contrast	Countdown
Decagram	Decontaminate	Decrease	Decay
Decease	Declassify	Decode	Defrost
Deforestation	Demography	Demoniac	De-monopolise
Demolition	Deport	Deprive	Dilemma
Demotion	Deportation	Discomfort	Decompose
Disconnect	Discount	Discontinue	Discourage
Disembody	Disengage	Disfavour	Disfigure
Disjoin	Dishonest	Disinfect	Disintegrate

Add the suitable prefixes to make new words:

coy	fraud	nude	valuate
crease	fray	nunciate	void
specialise	stock	supply	use
spend	strict	tax	value

purity	pound	polite	perturbable
pure	poverish	ponderable	petus
peach	practical	port	piety
accurate	capable	dellible	educable
action	compatible	delicate	effable

Chapter 13

Suffixes

A Suffix is a word placed at the end of a word to modify or change its meaning.
Suffixes can be classified on the basis of their meanings in the following dividsions though, some of them have more than one meaning.

Noun Suffixes are used in the formation of Abstract Nouns, such as:

~ age	frontage	mileage
~ ery	machinery	slavery
~ hood	manhood	brotherhood
~ ism	impressionism	nihilism
~ ship	partnership	friendship

Noun Suffixes are used in the formation of Concrete Nouns, such as:

~ eer	mountaineer	profiteer
~ er	villager	dresser
~ ess	actress	hostess
~ ette	cigarette	kitchenette
~ let	booklet	pamphlet

Noun Suffixes having a De-adjectival function, such as:

| ~ ism | classicism | romanticism |
| ~ ity | nicety | vulgarity |

Noun Suffixes having a De-verbal function, such as:

~ al	recital	survival
~ ant	assistant	participant
~ ation	examination	starvation
~ ee	examinee	employee
~ er	driver	reader

| ~ or | actor | supervisor |
| ~ ment | amazement | amusement |

Verb Suffixes having a De-nominal function, such as:

~ ate	hyphenate	orchestrate
~ fy	beautify	identify
~ ise	computerise	hospitalise

Verb Suffixes having a De-adjectival function, such as:

| ~ en | harden | soften |
| ~ ize | legalise | modernise |

An Adverb Suffix having a De-adjectival function, such as:

| ~ ly | foolishly | wisely |

Adverb Suffixes having a De-nominal function, such as:

| ~ ward/wards | homewards | southwards |
| ~ wise | nation-wise | population-wise |

Adjective Suffixes having a De-nominal function, such as:

~ al	magical	philosophical;
~ ed	diseased	talented
~ ful	peaceful	useful
~ ic	heroic	romantic
~ ih	childish	foolish
~ less	careless	homeless
~ ly	brotherly	motherly
~ ous	glamorous	humorous
~ worthy	praiseworthy	trustworthy
~ y	dusty	wealthy

Adjective Suffixes having a De-adjectival function, such as:

~ ly	deadly	sadly
~ al	economical	cynical
~ ish	greenish	whitish
~ some	gruesome	handsome

Adjective Suffixes having a De-adverbial function, such as:

| ~ able | drinkable | eatable |
| ~ ive | constructive | possessive |

Other Suffixes with Meanings and Examples:

Suffix	Meaning	Example	Example
~ able	capable of being	bearable	comfortable
~iac	pertaining to	cardiac	demonic
~ acity	quality of	tenacity	veracity
~ acy	having the quality of	fallacy	accuracy
~ ance	denoting state or action	assistance	abundance
~ ar	pertaining to	regular	angular
~ avian	referring to pursuits or doctrines	humanitarian	octogenarian
~ crat	ruler; member of the ruling body	autocrat	democrat
~ dom	power or state	wisdom	kingdom
~ ery	business or place of business	bakery	grocery
~ fic	making; causing; producing	prolific	pacific
~ gram	something drawn or written	diagram	monogram
~ hood	state; condition or nature	childhood	womanhood
~ ion	denotes action, progress, condition	confusion	opinion
~ ize. Ise	to make; to act	minimise	solemnise
~ ly	like	manly	mainly
~ lysis	decomposition; breaking down	paralysis	analysis

~ metry	art of measuring	
	geometry	trigonometry
~ our, or	action, state, condition	
	valour	labour
~ ose	full of; given to	
~ scape	scene, view	
	landscape	seascape
~ sy	state	
	courtesy	fantasy
~ ty	makes Abstract Nouns	
	levity	gravity
~ urgy	work	
	metallurgy	dramaturgy
~ ward, wards	direction	
	homeward	upward
~ way, ways, away	manner	
	highways	straightaway
~ y	diminutive	
	Baby	daddy

EXERCISES

Add ~ ate to the following letters to make new words:

b	c	d	f	g	h	l	m	p	r	s	t

Add ~ ate to the following group of words to make new words:

ab	deb	reb	devi	sati	ultim	dict
culmi	instig	accur	motiv	navig	radi	rot

Write the original words (not the letters given before ~ ate) to know how the suffixes change the complexion and meanings of the following words.

actuate	illustrate	innumerate
adequate	innovate	inoculate
aggregate	illuminate	un-ornate
aggravate	enumerate	inosculate
agitate	enunciate	inculcate
annotate	evaluate	inculpate
appreciate	negotiate	inadequate
appropriate	graduate	expatiate
alienate	mutilate	extricate
germinate	medicate	expatriate
terminate	bifurcate	expectorate
concentrate	compensate	commensurate
depreciate	complicate	frustrate
refocillate	commentate	frigate
replicate	fascinate	decimate
fulminate	operate	delegate
deflagrate	defalcate	denunciate
delicate	nominate	

Words Grow with Suffixes

Study the following words well which have one base word, **Cate** ~ *but have grown into more than forty words. Words grow, and grow fast with suffixes.*

cate	catechise	catechetic
catechetical	catechetically	catechetics
catechesis	catechiser	catechistic
catechistical	catechism	catechist
catechistic	catechsmal	catechu
catechol	catechumen	catechmate
catechumenical	catechumenically	catechumenism
catechumenship	categorical	categorically
categorical	categorematic	categoricalness
categorise	categorist	catelog; catalogue
catena	catenae	catenas
catenarian	catenavian	catenary
catenate	cateran	cate-cousin
caterpillar	caterwaul	caterer

Study the Suffix ~ ly.

~ **ly** is a Suffix of Adjectives which means like; having the characteristics of; or pertaining to; or occurring at a specified period

~ **ly** is a Suffix of Adverbs which means in a specified manner. It is used to form Adverbs from Adjectives. It also suggests occurring at every specified interval or period as for example: weekly, yearly, etc.

In case where an Adjective already ends in ~ ly, the form of the Adjective and the Adverb are often identical. They are separated obviously only by their use. For example:

  a kindly smile   Adjective

  to speak kindly   Adverb

Occasionally, ~ ly is added to ~ ly. The first ~ ly changes to **li** as in surlily, an awkward word to pronounce.

Separate the following words ending in ~ly into three different categories:

a. Adjectives

b. Adverbs

c. Words which are used as both Adjectives and Adverbs:

properly	timidly	monthly
worldly	earthly	daily

weekly	subtly	solemnly
simply	sweetly	silently
lovely	lovingly	gaily
gladly	godly	gravely
feebly	strongly	objectively
eagerly	beggarly	dangerously
effectively	foolishly	heavenly
humbly	highly	honestly
safely	costly	dearly
truly	avidly	seriously
severely	frankly	openly
rightly	wrongly	briefly
shortly	freely	wisely
graciously	badly	pitilessly
mercilessly	luckily	meticulously

Words with Suffix, ~logy.

~ logy means the science, or the study of, for example:

Word	Meanings
Analogy	The study of similarity
Anthology	A collection of choice
Anthropology	Study of man
Apology	regretful acknowledgement
Archeology	Study of antiquities
Astrology	Art of judging occult influence
Biology	Science of physical life
Morphology	Origin and distribution of animals and plants
Chronology	Science of computing dates
Criminology	Science of crime and criminology
Ethnology	Science of races
Etymology	Study of formation and meaning of words
Geneology	Accounts of ancestry
Herpetology	Study of reptiles

Iconology	Study of images, etc
Litho logy	Science of stones
Martyrology	Study of martyrs
Meteorology	Study of weather
Mycology	Study of fungi
Climatology	Study of climate
Mycology	Science of muscles
Mythology	Study of traditional stories
Nosology	Science of classification of diseases
Ontology	Study of abstract beings
Ornithology	Study of birds
Osteology	Study of bones
Pathology	Study of bodily diseases
Phonology	Science of sound
Phraseology	Study of words and expressions
Phrenology	Study of mental faculty
Physiology	Study of living organisms
Pomo logy	Science of fruits
Psychology	Science of mind and behavior
Technology	Science of industry/industries
Terminology	Science of the use of terms
Theology	Study of religion
Triology	Study of plays
Zoology	Study of living beings

Separate the suffixes from the words given below:

kingdom	terrorise	durable
candy	symmetry	hairy
minority	northward	snobbish
freedom	familiar	poetic
peripheral	scholarly	communion
filthy	peaceful	sonogram
adulthood	vainly	heresy
useful	accidental	polar
musical	robbery	flattery

zealous	heroic	always
revise	chubby	martyrdom
opinion	wealthy	boyhood
terror	optometry	diplomacy
zodiac	honour	fusion
distance	poisonous	aristocrat
trivial	finery	womanly
comfortable	downward	terror

Words with the Suffix ~ ist

amorist	armorist	alchemist
anatomist	antagonist	anarchist
botanist	bigamist	chiropodist
fatalist	gastronomist	horticulturist
lepidopterist	masochist	philanthropist
specialist	spiritualist	embryologist
orthodontist	periodontist	prosthetist
optimist	pessimist	futurist
nudist	metalist	taxidermist
zoophilist	occulist	dramatist
melodramatist	sentimentalist	atheist
theist	internist	therapentist
allergist	misogamist	anesthetist
optometrist	podiatrist	dentist
evodontist	prosthadontist	extremist
geologist	gynecologist	finalist
dermatologist	semantologist	morphologist

Words with the Suffix ~ ous

tenuous	sumptuous	luminous
spacious	serious	glorious
ridiculous	credulous	sensuous
previous	obvious	various
preposterous	dexterous	incongruous
ominous	slanderous	vigorous

luminous	vivacious	delicious
licentious	lascivious	surreptitious
illustrious	judicious	capacious
gorgeous	voluptuous	lecherous
frivolous	treacherous	tremendous
curious	furious	spurious
ceremonious	tenacious	luxurious

Words with Suffix ~ ment

The Suffix ~ment stands for means or instrument for action or state resulting from action.

agreement	abridgement	argument
arrangement	atonement	attachment
bombardment	contentment	development
determent	discernment	disillusionment
detachment	endearment	enjoyment
entertainment	enforcement	enrichment
fragment	figment	fulfillment
firmament	franchisement	government
harassment	improvement	implement
investment	internment	impediment
judgment	management	merriment
movement	ornament	payment
procurement	prepayment	placement
refinement	requirement	resentment
shipment	statement	sacrament
segment	sentiment	alignment
abasement	abridgement	testament
vehement	increment	deploment

Words with the Suffix ~ fy

amplify	calcify	classify
fructify	falsify	gratify
justify	magnify	nullify
petrify	qualify	ratify
rectify	stultify	signify
specify	simplify	acidify

electrify	diversify	identify
personify	defy	deify
dignify	vivify	prettify

Separate the Suffixes from the words given below and write the base words

successful	legislature	directorate
manager	supervisor	forgetful
sandy	managerial	deadly
educational	normalcy	selfish
bravery	selfishness	description
dialectical	restless	unexpectedly
actor	piglet	picturesque
hesitation	reducible	compensate
loyalty	government	usually
poetic	driver	eventful
professorship	psychological	Miltonic
devotional	Johnsonian	relativity
delightful	retirement	windy
versification	historic	possibility
signify	functional	significant
verification	senseless	outlet
disciplinarian	humorous	homely

More words with the Suffix ~ logy

Desology	Posology	Etiology
Pathology	Nosology	Physiology
Symptomatology	Semology	Serology
Taxicology	Somatology	Histology
Anesthesiology	Epidermiology	Immunology
Virology	Tocology	Gyneology

Words with the Suffix ~ phobia

~ phobia means the fear of

Phobias and their Meanings

Words	**Meanings**
Methyphobia	The fear of alcohol
Autophobia	The fear of loneliness
Myronecophobia	The fear of ants

Phobias and their Meanings

Words	Meanings
Apiphobia	The fear of bees
Hemophobia	The fear of blood
Gephyrophobia	The fear of bridge
Betaphobia	The fear of buildings
Claustrophobia	The fear from being confined to a place
Amaxophobia	The fear of cars
Agyrophobia	The fear of crossing a street
Lygophobia	The fear of dark places
Arachnophobia	The fear of darkness
Musophobia	The fear of mice
Demophobia	The fear of crows
Thalassophobia	The fear of ocean
Scoleciphobia	The fear of worms
Arachnophobia	The fear of spiders
Thanatophobia	The fear of dying
Dentophobia	The fear of a dentist
Ophidiophobia	The fear of small creatures like snake
Bathophobia	The fear from depth
Electrophobia	The fear from electricity
Arsonphobia	The fear of fire
Ichthyphobia	The fear of fish
Felinophobia	The fear of cat
Anthrophobia	The fear of flowers
Aviophobia	The fear of flying
Xenophobia	The fear of foreigners
Doraphobia	The fear of animal skin
Aerophobia	The fear of heights
Nosocomephobia	The fear of hospitals
Lyponophobia	The fear of injections
Acousticophobia	The fear of noise
Herpetophobia	The fear of ripple
Hydrophobia	The fear from water
Chionophobia	The fear from snow
Aichmophobia	The fear of sharp objects
Agoiaphobia	The fear of crowded places

Phobias and their Meanings

Words	Meanings
Altophobia	The fear of heights
Nomenophobia	The fear of brands
Senecophobia	The fear of growing old
Bulliphobia	The fear of not having the remote control
Cadophobia	The fear of failure
Calvophobia	The fear of going bald
Canusophobia	The fear of going grey
Civiliphobia	The fear of politicians
Donoculophobia	The fear of eye contact
Duxophobia	The fear of your boss
Frigensophobia	The fear of using your mobile
Illerogophobia	The fear of the unanswerable questions
Inanophobia	The fer of being put on hold
Laudophobia	The fear of fans
Malvocophobia	The fear of using wrong words
Uxorphobia	The fear of one's wife
Scalaphobia	The fear of escalators
Saltaphobia	The fear of dancing
Necrophobia	The fear of corpses
Hygrophobia	The fear of dampness
Traumatophobia	The fear of injury
Hapaxophobia	The fear of robber
Amychophobia	The fear of scratches
Ophidiophobia	The fear of snake
Laliophobia	The fear of speaking
Chronophobia	The fear of time
Hodophobia	The fear of travel
Amaxophobia	The fear of vehicle
Basiphobia	The fear of walking
Gynophobia	The fear of women
Cynophobia	The fear of dogs
Phagophobia	The fear of eating
Kakorrhaphiophobia	The fear of failure
Iatrophobia	The fear of doctors
Antlophobia	The fear of floods

Phobias and their Meanings

Words	Meanings
Homichlophobia	The fear of fog
Batrachophobia	The fear of frogs
Hylophobia	The fear of forest
Phasmophobia	The fear of ghosts
Parthenophobia	The fear of girls
Graphophobia	The fear of writing
Aichmophobia	The fear of knife
Pediculophobia	The fear of lice
Astraphobia	The fear of lightning
Gamophobia	The fear of marriage
Pharmacophobia	The fear of medicine
Chrematophobia	The fear of money
Onomatophobia	The fear of name
Osmophobia	The fear of odour
Agoraphobia	The fear of open spaces
Ponophobia	The fear of work
Algophobia	The fear of pain
Siderodromophobia	The fear of railroad or train
Hypengyophobia	The fear of responsibility
Thermophobia	The fear of heat
Categelophobia	The fear of ridicule
Potamophobia	The fear of river

Words with Suffix ~ ute which means do or lessen

commute	constitute	convolute
depute	dispute	electrocute
execute	impute	permute
compute	pollute	persecute
prosecute	substitute	attribute
contribute	tribute	distribute

Words with Suffix ~ ator

annotator	calculator	duplicator	lubricator
conservator	elevator	operator	creator
escalator	generator	curator	dilator

incubator	demonstrator	translator	spectator

Words with Suffix ~ee

addressee	absentee	referee	repartee
appointee	devotee	refugee	matinee
examinee	payee		

Words with Suffix ~tory

isolatory	hortatory	ditonatory	derogatory
promptory	diliatory	dictator	dissimilatory
deprecatory	defamatory	laboratory	mandatory

Words with Suffix ~ ine

theophiline	tuperine	cinchonine	emetine
tuborcurarine	rinblastine	ephedrine	ergotamine
vincrtrine	yohimbine	gallamine	morphine
resperine	berberine	muscarine	histamine
bicuculine	caffeine	quinidine	quinine

Words with Suffix ~ ia

acadaemia	anaemia	dyspepsia	asthenopia
eupepria	amblyopia	diplopia	ammonia
amblyopia	myopia	hernia	insomnia

Words with Suffix ~ ant

instant	constant	distant	blatant

Words with Suffix ~ archy

oligarchy	anarchy	triarchy	pentarchy
monarchy	duarchy	tetrarchy	

Words with Suffix ~ cian

mathematician	arithmetician	phonetician	politician
electrician	geometrician	tactician	technician
obstetrician	optician		

Pormanteau Words

Besides these, there are words that we use in our day-to-day life which are formed by merging the sounds and meanings of two different words.

Advertainment	advertisement + entertainment
Affluenza	affluence + influenza
Because	by + cause
Bionic	biology + electronic
Bit	binary + digit
Brunch	Breakfast + lunch
Cellophane	cellulose + diaphane
Diabesity	diabetes + obesity
Email	electronic + mail
Fantabulous	fantastic + fabulous
Fortnight	fourteen + nights
Globish	global + English
Goodby	God+be(with)+ye
Hinglish	Hindi + English
Infotainment	information+entertainment
Intercom	internal + communication
Internet	international + network
Knowledgebase	knowledge + database
Modem	modulator + demodulator
Seascape	sea + landscape
Smog	smoke + fog
Soundscape	sound + landscape
Telegenic	television + photogenic
Telex	teleprinter + monologue
Travelogue	travel + monologue
Webinar	web + seminar
Zonkey	Zebra + donkey

Phile Words

'Phile': Words pertaining to the love of something.

acrophile	a lover of mountains
aerophilatelist	one who collects air-mail stamps
anglophile	a lover of England and/or the English
cartophily	the collecting of cigarette cards
discophily	the collecting of gramophone records

peridromophily	the collecting of bus and railway tickets
philanthrope	a lover of mankind
zoophilist	a lover of animals

Miso words

MISO-Words pertaining to the hate of something.

misanthrope	a hater of mankind
misocapnik	one who hates cigarette smoking
misogamist	one who hates marriage
misogynist	a person who hates women
misologist	one who hates learning or knowledge

Mania words

Mania: An obsession to do something.

anthomania	a great lover of flowers
bibliokleptomania	a mental aberration leading to the stealing of books
dipsomania	the compulsion to drink alcohol
pyromania	the compulsion to start fires

Others

aesthetics	relating to the study or appreciation of beauty
aficionado	a keen follower of a sport
alopecia	baldness
amnesia	loss of memory
anorexia	loss of appetite
capnomancy	divination from smoke
cartomancy	divination from playing cards
cheironomy	the science of expression by means of gestures
dyslexia	word blindness
misandy	a morbid fear of men by women
phonocamptics	the study of echoes
pyrotechnics	fireworks
syndrome	a set of symptoms

Chapter 14

Antonyms: Opposites

Antonyms are words that have opposite (or nearly opposite) meanings. For example: *up-down, day-night*, etc.

Opposite Words

above	below; beneath	antipathy	sympathy
absence	presence	appreciate	deprecate
accept	deny; refuse; reject	appear	disappear
abundance	scarcity	arrival	departure
accuse	defend	ascend	descend
active	indolent	ascent	descent
add	subtract	assist	hinder
admit	deny	asleep	awake
admire	despise	attack	defend
advance	retard	attentive	careless
advance	arrear	attract	repel
adverse	favourable	alive	dead
adversity	prosperity	amateur	professional
advantage	disadvantage	assemble	disperse
affirmative	negative	back	front
after	before	backward	forward
against	for	barbarous	civilised
agree	differ; disagree	barren	fertile
all	none	beautiful	ugly
allow	disallow	begin	end
always	never	belief	distrust
answer	question	believe	doubt
ancient	modern	benefit	harm
analysis	synthesis	bogus	genuine

borrow	lend	diligent	idle; lazy
both	neither	domestic;	foreign; wild
brave	timid	dwarf	giant
bright	dull; stupid	efficient	unskilled
calm	disturbed	enemy	ally
cause	effect	enough	insufficient
care	neglect	entrance	exit
chaos	order	expense	income
chaste	corrupt	expert	novice
cheap	dear	export	import
cheerful	cheerless	extravagant	frugal
common	rare	exclude	include
comedy	tragedy	examiner	examinee
concave	convex	fail	succeed
condemn	approve	faithful	faithless
confess	deny	floor	ceiling
confirm	annul	foolish	sensible; wise
continue	cease	fortune	misfortune
create	destroy	freedom	slavery
credit	cash	forefather	descendent
deep	shallow	forgive	punish
debtor	creditor	friendly	hostile
decent	indecent	general	particular
demand	supply	grief	joy
demon; devil	angel	guile	honest
despair	hope	guilty	innocent
detach	attach	hard	soft
difficult	easy	haste	delay
defeat	win	heaven	hell
deficit	surplus	heavy	light
dissatisfied	content	height	depth
deposit	withdraw	help	hinder
dependent	independent	hollow	solid
defendant	plaintiff	humble	proud
destructive	constructive; creative	illegal	lawful

illiterate	learned	negative	positive
impossible	likely	normal	abnormal
increase	decrease	noble	ignoble
inhale	exhale	obey	disobey
initial	final	offer	refuse
inferior	superior	offend	please
inflation	deflation	optional	compulsory
inside	outside	optimistic	pessimistic
interior	exterior	ordinary	unique
interesting	insipid; boring	oral	written
just	earnest	partner	rival
junior	senior	pass	fail
justice	injustice	peace	war
kind	cruel	please	displease
lad	lass	penalty	reward
lament	rejoice	persuade	dissuade
lean	fat	permanent	temporary
liabilities	assets	permission	prohibition
like	detest; dislike	polished	rough
limited	infinite	practice	theory
liquid	solid; gas	praise	defame
loyal	disloyal	primary	secondary
lovely	hideous	private	public
lenient	strict	punctual	late
make	mar	pure	impure; polluted
material	spiritual	progress	retrogression
maximum	minimum	raw	ripe
means	end	real	imaginary
monarch	subject	recovery	relapse
much	less	respect	contempt
mortal	immortal	revenge	forgiveness
merit	demerit	robust	delicate
modest	immodest	rude	polite
moveable	immovable	remember	forget
natural	artificial	rural	urban

savage	civilised	unique	common
sharp	blunt	universal	parochial
similar	different	utility	futility
sour	sweet	vain	modest
show	hide	vague	definite
spend	save	voice	virtue
suffix	prefix	victory	defeat
tame	wild	villain	hero
teacher	pupil	virile	effeminate
tragedy	comedy	voluntary	compulsory
treacherous	faithful	wealth	poverty
transparent	opaque	wicked	virtuous
uniform	varied	wisdom	folly

Multiple Opposites

Abandon:	continue	pursue	remain	carry on
Above:	below	down	under	
Abolish:	confirm	uphold	promote	encourage
Ability:	incompetence	incompetency	disability	incapacity
Abridge:	enlarge	prolong	expand	magnify
Absolve:	punish	chastise	castigate	penalise
Absurd:	wise	rational	sensible	reasonable
Abundance:	lack	dearth	shortage	want
Acquit:	charge	blame	accuse	involve
Adapt:	differ	misfit	disagree	irregularity
Admiration:	hate	condemnation	disapproval	
Ample:	meager	scanty	insufficient	limited
Amuse:	annoy	fatigue	tire	bore
Atrocious:	noble	excellent	worthy	laudable
Attract:	reject	repulse	repel	rebuff
Awake:	asleep	dormant	latent	slumbering
Backward:	forward	advance	onward	prompt
Beautiful:	ugly	hideous	loathsome	horrible
Before:	after	subsequently	succeeding	
Belief:	disbelief	suspicious	misgiving	distrust
Benevolence:	malice	venom	enmity	hate

Beseech:	challenge	demand	content	insist
Bewilder:	illuminate	edify	enlighten	
Bitter:	mellow	genial	sweet	honeyed
Blame:	praise	applaud	complement	extol
Bliss:	sorrow	affliction	woe	distress
Bold:	afraid	fearful	timid	different
Breed:	destroy	kill	murder	annihilate
Brutal:	humane	tender	compassionate	merciful
Bright:	opaque	cloudy	dull	dark
Brief:	long	detailed	verbose	diffused
Busy:	inactive	lazy	indolent	idle
Calamity:	fortune	peace	happiness	joy
Calm:	excited	perturbed	agitated	disturbed
Cancel:	confirm	accept	establish	endorse
Careless:	cautious	vigilant	attentive	heedful
Certain:	dubious	doubtful	obscure	ambiguous
Charm:	repulsive	repellent	deter	rebuff
Cheerful:	torpid	lifeless	inert	sluggish
Claim:	renounce	forgo	waive	abandon
Coarse	smooth	polite	refined	cultured
Cold:	fiery	tepid	warm	scalding
Compel:	coax	cajole	dissuade	discourage
Competent:	incompetent	inefficient	weak	naïve
Compliment:	criticism	censure	disapprobation	comment
Confide:	distrust	apprehend	doubt	suspect
Dainty:	coarse	vulgar	crude	rough
Defeat:	triumph	vanquish	prevail	win
Decide:	hesitate	vacillate	waver	falter
Delicious:	repulsive	abhorrent	tasteless	distasteful
Delight:	grief	anguish	displeasure	sorrow
Deny:	verify	confirm	comply	endorse
Deviate:	abide	persist	converge	loathe
Diligent:	idle	slack	lazy	loathsome
Disclose:	conceal	veil	cloak	hide
Disgust:	please	delight	charm	gratify
Dishonest:	reliable	just	fair	trustworthy
Dispute:	consent	comply	agree	accept

Dutiful:	defiant	rebellious	revolting	seditious
Enchanted:	disgusted	repulsed	nauseated	disillusioned
Encourage:	discourage	dampen	depress	dishearten
Endanger:	protected	defended	shield	safeguard
Entice:	rebuff	repel	deter	repulse
Establish:	destroy	dismantle	demolish	disfigure
Everlasting:	temporal	mortal	transitory	transient
Expand:	contract	condense	curtail	reduce
Extraordinary	normal	ordinary	common	usual
False:	true	verified	accurate	authentic
Famous:	obscure	notorious	unknown	anonymous
Feeble:	robust	strong	vigorous	powerful
Fertile:	sterile	unfertile	arid	barren
Flexible:	rigid	stiff	austere	unbending
Foe:	ally	comrade	colleague	associate
Foolish:	wise	sane	discreet	rational
Generous:	mean	stingy	miserly	parsimonious
Gloomy:	merry	jolly	jocund	joyous
Graceful:	awkward	ungainly	graceless	pliable
Great:	common	trivial	unknown	superfluous
Happiness:	sorrow	sadness	grief	distress
Hard:	soft	smooth	flexible	pliable
Hasten:	impede	retard	hinder	delay
Hatred:	love	liking	affection	adoration
Hesitate:	decide	resolve	settle	determine
Horrible:	agreeable	pleasant	delightful	charming
Humble:	vain	proud	brazen	immodest
Ignorant:	cultured	educated	literate	knowledgeable
Impartial:	partial	biased	unjust	unfair
Impede:	expedite	hasten	quicken	urge
Impulsive:	cautious	heedful	thoughtful	reasonable
Innocent:	wicked	guilty	criminal	culprit
Irritate:	calm	appease	soothe	pacify
Jolly:	gloomy	dismal	unhappy	sad
Just:	unfair	prejudiced	biased	partial
Kind:	cruel	hard	harsh	callous
Kill:	create	invent	produce	originate

Lead:	mislead	misguide	misdirect	deceive
Liberty:	slavery	service	bondage	submission
Mild:	savage	wild	fierce	ferocious
Muscular:	feeble weak	frail	infirm	
Narrow:	wide	spacious	broad	extensive
Neat:	untidy	disorderly	slovenly	
Nervous:	bold fearless	valiant	undaunted	
Obedient:	obstinate	stubborn	revolting	
Oppose:	aid assist	encourage	support	
Organise:	disorganise	disrupt	disarrange	disintegrate
Passionate:	cold	impassive	torpid	dispassionate
Pathetic:	funny	comic	ludicrous	farcical
Peevish:	cordial	jovial	genial	hearty
Prolong:	curtail	dismissal	decrease	shorten
Puzzle:	solution	clear	explanation	elucidation
Quarrel:	accede	consent	comply	acquiesce
Quick:	slow	lethargic	inactive	sloth
Rash:	careful	heedful	discreet	cautious
Real:	fanciful	dreamy	imaginary	illusive
Remove:	restore	rehabilitate	supersede	reinstate
Rival:	friend	chum	intimate	ally
Rude:	civil	polite	courteous	genteel
Sacred:	profane	irreligious	irreverent	impious
Selfish:	generous	liberal	lavish	charitable
Shy:	bold	confident	audacious	assuming
Steady:	irregular	inconsistent	unstable	fickle
Suppress:	excite	provoke	incite	agitate
Talkative:	taciturn	reserved	silent	mute
Tear:	repair	mend	rectify	restore
Try:	quit	abandon	relinquish	drop
Yield:	withhold	restrain	suppress	detain
Zenith:	nadir	bottom	bases	base

Chapter 15

Synonyms: Similar in Meaning

These are words or phrases which mean exactly or nearly the same as other words or phrases in the same language. For example: the synonyms of *Beautiful-pretty, lovely, gorgeous, ravishing, stunning*, etc.

Multiple Synonyms

Adaptation:	conformation	harmonisation	matching	synchronization
Apt:	appropriate	applicable	germane	pertinent
Adjust:	accommodate	adapt	attune	confirm
Accelerate:	energise	intensify	stimulate	step-up
All:	aggregate	gross	sum	total
Accumulation:	agglomeration	aggregation	concentration	conglomeration
Accuse:	blacken	culminate	denigrate	malign
Abnormal:	aberrant	anomalous	eccentric	freakish
Apathetic:	unambitious	unenthusiastic	uninspired	unmoved
Abode:	dwelling	home	residence	living-place
Adieu:	farewell	goodbye	valediction	separation
Bate:	deduct	decrease	diminish	lessen
Bond:	yoke	chain	liaison	link
Bedevil:	confuse	confound	complicate	entangle
Bizarre:	funny	grotesque	odd	queer
Barbaric:	brutish	primitive	savage	wild
Behavior:	conduct	demeanour	deportment	
Breeze:	gale	wind	zephyr	
Beseech:	attractiveness	charm	elegance	grace
Bandit:	dacoit	robber	plagiarist	sea-plunderer
Bemoan:	grieve	lament	moan	weep-over

Circumstance:	condition	situation	factor	environment
Copy:	facsimile	replica	tracing	reproduction
Connect:	annex	attach	clip	contact
Constitute:	form	compose	organise	construct
Complex:	complicated	intricate	involved	winding
Contend:	combat	campaign	strive	tussle
Cooperation:	amity	compatibility	reciprocity	sympathy
Competent:	capable	clever	efficient	learned
Discontinue:	intervene	interrupt	interpose	interject
Divine:	celestial	numinous	sacred	sanctified
Degrading:	derogatory	demeaning	ignominious	lowering
Defiant:	disobedient	militant	proud	provocative
Disfigure:	cripple	deface	deform	maim
Damn:	curse	denounce	scold	swear
Deceit:	bluff	fraud	guile	knavery
Deity:	God	Goddess	Omnipotent	Providence
Demise:	death	decease	expire	eternal rest
Devoid:	empty	exempt from	immune from	release
Existence:	absoluteness	being	life	living
Ethnic:	racial	tribal	phyletic	clannish
Equilibrium:	balance	equipoise	poise	steadiness
Enormous:	colossal	immense	monumental	vast
Ending:	conclusive	final	terminal	ultimate
Endorse:	enact	enforce	legislate	ordain
Enrage:	anger	annoy	irritate	upset
Elevation:	culmination	eminence	loftiness	sublimity
Fragmentary:	broken	brushy	crumbly	in pieces
First:	initial	natal	original	starting
Forgiving:	condoning	forbearing	palpable	uneventful
Fatigue:	exhaust	exertion	grind	overtax
Friction:	interference	interruption	intervention	interception
Frigid:	biting	chilly	cold	shivering
Group:	cluster	flock	team	unit
Grave:	sedate	serious	sober	solemn
Greed:	avidity	lust	covetousness	rapacity
Generous:	bountiful	liberal	magnanimous	charitable

Hymn:	anthem	psalm	paean	eulogy
Hypocrite:	amoral	disloyal	traitor	treason
Hindrance:	barrier	hampering	impediment	obstruction
Heap:	collect	pile	gather	store
Join:	assemble	bracket	conjoin	council
Lenient:	palpable	mild	tender	tolerant
Natural:	normal	usual	consistent	regular
Man:	masculine	manful	stout	virile
Marriage:	matrimony	wedlock	alliance	nuptial tie
Musical:	melodious	melodic	tuneful	mellifluous
Messenger:	envoy	emissary	herald	harbinger
Mixture:	composite	alloy	amalgam	infusion
Moral:	ethical	virtuous	righteous	upright
Motivate:	drive	induce	persuade	provoke
Narrow:	slender	thin	slim	limited
Number:	symbol	numeral	digit	integer
Offer:	bid	proposal	proposition	motion
Opinion:	concept	view	notion	conclusion
Owner:	proprietor	partner	landlord	landholder
Partition:	division	section	branch	segment
Pity:	compassion	mercy	humanity	grace
Power:	potency	puissance	vigor	energy
Quake:	shake	tremble	quiver	shiver
Queer:	eccentric	abnormal	whimsical	quaint
Reasoning:	thinking	analysis	induction	inference
Result:	effect	consequence	aftermath	product
Search:	pursuit	quest	chase	exploration
Statement:	utterance	comment	manifesto	pronouncement
Story:	narrative	tale	legend	myth
Surprise:	amaze	astonish	astound	dumbfound
Vice:	infirmity	frailty	demerit	sin
Veracity:	reality	honesty	truthfulness	frankness
Zero:	naught	nil	cipher	nihil
Zenith:	summit	acme	pinnacle	apex

Chapter 16

Homonyms: Homophones

Words which may be spelled the same and may sound the same, but have different meanings.

peace	⇨	piece	bridal	⇨	bridle
pour	⇨	power	corps	⇨	corpse
obvious	⇨	oblivious	differ	⇨	defer
profit	⇨	prophet	hart	⇨	heart
dose	⇨	doze	minor	⇨	miner
pray	⇨	prey	blue	⇨	blew
story	⇨	storey	bore	⇨	boar
vain	⇨	vein; vane	stair	⇨	stare
scene	⇨	sin; seen	dual	⇨	duel; duet
altar	⇨	alter	check	⇨	cheque
cattle	⇨	kettle	assay	⇨	essay
dear	⇨	deer	avocation	⇨	vocation
canvas	⇨	canvass	amiable	⇨	amicable
mail	⇨	male	sail	⇨	sell; sale; cell
preposition	⇨	proposition	suite	⇨	suit
root	⇨	rout; route	steal	⇨	steel; still
fair	⇨	fare	tenor	⇨	tenure
pain	⇨	pane	tell	⇨	tail; tale
soul	⇨	sole	umpire	⇨	empire
main	⇨	mane;	veil	⇨	vale
read	⇨	reed	accident	⇨	incident
way	⇨	weigh	artist	⇨	artiste; artisan
born	⇨	borne	appose	⇨	oppose

soar	⇨	sore; sour	major	⇨	measure
confess	⇨	suppress	divest	⇨	invest
jealous	⇨	zealous	coir	⇨	choir
ghastly	⇨	ghostly	facilitate	⇨	felicitate
averse	⇨	adverse	edible	⇨	eatable
evolve	⇨	devolve; involve	statute	⇨	statue

Words that We Generally Confuse (Confusables)

ability	power to do something	**affectation**	unnatural feeling
capacity	power to receive	**album**	a book of photos
ablution	ceremonial washing	**albumen**	the white of an egg
washing	general washing	**alienate**	to withdraw affection
abnormal	deviation from usual	**allineate**	to bring into line
subnormal	inferior to usual	**already**	by this time
accelerate	increase the speed	**all ready**	fully ready
exhilarate	make cheerful	**alternate**	by turns
accept	agree to take	**alternative**	to offer choice
except	omit	**analyst**	skilled in analysis
access	chance of getting	**annalist**	the writer of annals
excess	immoderateness	**apprise**	to inform
accessory	intentional aid	**apprize**	to evaluate
accessory	additional	**assume**	suppose
acquire	to develop power	**presume**	take for granted
acquisition	material gains	**autarchy**	sovereignty
addicted	bad qualities	**autarky**	self sufficiency
devoted	good qualities	**cavalry**	mounted militancy
adherence	sticking to qualities	**calvary**	the place of crucifixion
adhesion	sticking fast	**censor**	examine before allowing
adapt	adjust properly	**censure**	to criticise unfavourably
adopt	to treat as one's own	**climactic**	climax
advent	momentous arrival	**climatic**	climate
arrival	physical presence	**collaborate**	work together
affect	to cause	**decent**	proper and suitable
change	effect to bring result	**descent**	downward movement

affection	kind feeling	**egoism**	philosophical theory
egotism	indulgence in self praise	**loose**	lack of control
emigrant	leaves a country	**lose**	to suffer deprivation
immigrant	comes to a country	**metal**	an article
enervate	weakening	**mettle**	a spirit
innervate	to invigorate	**moral**	teaching
entomology	study of insects	**morale**	discipline
etymology	study of words	**motif**	theme
epical	pertaining to epic	**motive**	intention
epochal	new period of time	**oral**	using speech
ethical	related to ethics	**aural**	related to ears
ethnical	related to study of rules	**personnel**	persons employed
extent	size, measure	**personal**	relating to one person
extant	still in existence	**precede**	to come before
hail	greet	**proceed**	go on
hale	healthy	**premier**	prime minister
hoard	save and store up	**premiere**	first show of a film
horde	a tribal crowd	**prescribe**	designated
insolate	expose to sunlight	**proscribe**	prohibited
insulate	insolate electricity	**pursue**	seek after
irruption	a sudden and violent entry	**peruse**	read carefully
eruption	bursting forth	**sensible**	reasonable
liquidity	make or become liquid	**sensitive**	easily affected
liquidate	exterminate		

Chapter 17

Acronyms

The term, **acronyms** an abbreviation formed from the initial components in a phrase or a word. These components may be individual letters (as in CEO) or parts of words (as in *Benelux* and *Ameslan*).

The spelled out form of an acronym (that is what it stands for) is called its expansion. Some words are pronounced as a word containing only the initial letters.

AIDS: Acquired Immune Deficiency Syndrome.

NATO: North Atlantic Treaty Organisation

Some words are pronounced as a word containing non- initial letters.

1. Interpol: International Criminal Police Organization
2. Nabisco: National Biscuit Company
3. Radar: Radio Detection and Ranging

Some words are pronounced as the nouns of letters.

1. BBC: British Broadcasting Corporation
2. USA: The United States of America
3. IRA: The Irish Republican Army

Some other acronyms are:-

1. G.I. – Government Issue
2. G.M.T – Greenwich Mean Time
3. G.N.P – Gross National Profit
4. G.P. – General Practitioner
5. H.Q. – Head Quarters
6. I.M.F. – Indian Monetary Fund

Some Useful and Important Acronyms

1. R.S.V.P – Response If You Please
2. E.S.L. – English as a Second Language
3. E.F.L – English as a Foreign Language

P.M/A.M

P.M. is also written as p.m. which means

Post - Meridian (Afternoon)

A.M is also written as a.m. which means Ante-Meridian (Before noon)

1. C.C.T.V – Closed Circuit Television
2. C.D – Compact Disc
3. C.I.A – Central Intelligence Agency
4. D.V.D – Digital Video Disc
5. E.S.P.N – Entertainment and Sports Programming Network
6. F.B.I- Federal Bureau of Investigation
7. P.O.W – Prisoner of War
8. P.R. – Public Relations
9. RIP – Rest in Peace
10. TA – Teaching Assistant
11. T.B. Tuberculosis
12. T.B.A – To Be Announced

Chapter 18

Abbreviations

We live in an era of continuous oral and written expressions. There are certain words or a combination of words which can be abbreviated or shortened by writing just the first letter of the word. For example: *NATO (North Atlantic Treaty Organisation), WHO (World Health Organisation)*, etc.

Some Common Abbreviations	
BISLY	But I Still Love You
BFF	Best friends, forever!
TTYL	Talk To You Later
IIRC	If I Recall Correctly...
AFAIK	As Far as I Know
WRT	With Respect To
NWT	New With Tags
OTOH	On the Other Hand
AFK	Away from Keyboard
ASL	Age/Sex/Location?
TPTB	The Powers that Be
IMHO	In My Humble Opinion
OATUS	On a Totally Unrelated Subject
PMFJI	Pardon Me for Jumping In
SFSG	So Far, So Good
TC	Take Care!
O RLY	Oh, Really (sarcasm)
OP	The Original Poster (who started this discussion thread)
WB	Welcome Back
IDK	I Don't Know

LBW	Love and best wishes
MEGO	My Eyes Glaze Over
SASA	Short and Sweet Reply
YMMV	Your Mileage May Vary
MTFBWY	May the Force Be With You
NIMBY	Not in My Back Yard
MT	Mistell (mistaken chat message, please disregard)
KISS	Keep it short and simple

Words Denoting Etiquettes	
NETHICS	Ethics on the net
BRB	Be Right Back
ACK	Acknowledged
HTH	"Hope this helps" "Happy to help"
HAND	Have a nice day

Chapter 19

One-word Substitutes

One Word for Many Words

Agenda	Item of business to be considered at a meeting
Aggressor	One who attacks first
Anarchist	One who plans to destroy all governments
Arbitrator	one appointed by parties to settle disputes
Amateur	one who does something for pleasure
Antidote	A medicine to nullify the effect of poison
Atheist	One who does not believe in the existence of God
Autobiography	A life-history of a man written by himself
Autocracy	Government by one person
Bankrupt	Unable to pay one's debts; insolvent
Bibliography	List of books read or consulted
Bigot	One with narrow religious views
Bigamy	The state of having two wives or husbands at a time
Biography	The life-history of a person written by another person
Bilingual	One who speaks two languages
Bureaucracy	Governments by officials
Cannibal	One who eats human flesh
Catalogue	List of books or other articles
Carnivorous	One who eats flesh
Credulous	One who easily believes
Colleagues	Those who work in the same office or department
Celibacy	The state of being without a mate
Cemetry	A place of burial
Contemporary	Living in the same age

Cosmopolitan	Of/from different parts of the world
Democracy	Government by the representatives of the people
Diplomacy	The art practised by statesmen
Drought	Want of rain; dry state
Elementary	That which is basic
Emigrant	One who leaves one's country to settle elsewhere
Egoist	A man who thinks only of himself
Epidemic	A disease that spreads over a large area
Exchange	Giving and receiving
Extempore	Speech without any preparation
Exultant	Feeling or show of great pride
Facsimile	An exact copy of something
Fanatic	A person extremely enthusiastic about something
Fascism	An extreme right-wing political system
Fantastic	Extremely beautiful, praiseworthy
Fastidious	Hard to satisfy
Fratricide	Killing of one's brother
Foreigner	A man who is not the citizen of the country
Gullible	One who is too willing to believe
Glossary	A list of technical or special words
Glutton	A person who eats too much
Genetics	The study of the characteristics of generations
Geology	Scientific study of the Earth
Holistic	Belief in being more than a collection of parts
Honorary	An office without a pay
Homicide	Killing of a man
Herbivorous	Animals living on grass and herbs
Horoscope	A study of the effects of the stars and planets on life
Inaccessible	That which cannot be approached
Inaudible	That which cannot be heard
Ineligible	Not qualified to be elected or selected under rules
Inexplicable	That which cannot be explained
Illegible	That which cannot be read
Introvert	He who remains busy in himself
Invisible	That which cannot be seen

Illiterate	One who can neither read nor write
Invincible	That which cannot be won
Incorrigible	That which cannot be corrected
Inimitable	That which cannot be imitated
Indispensible	That without which one cannot do
Inevitable	That which cannot be avoided
Incurable	That which cannot be cured
Irrevocable	That which cannot be changed
Irritable	Easily excited to anger
Irrelevant	That which is not to the point
Incredible	That which cannot be believed
Infallible	That which cannot fail
Inflammable	Liable to catch fire easily
Insecticide	A medicine that kills insects
Invulnerable	That which cannot be hurt
Irrepressible	That which cannot be checked
Illegal	Against law
Illicit	A trade prohibited by law
Ignominy	Public shame and loss of honour
Irruption	Sudden and violent entry
Intimacy	Very close relationship
Itinerary	A detailed plan of a journey
Judiciary	Pertaining to the judges of a country
Kidnap	To take away illegally
Kinship	The fact of being related in a family
Labyrinth	A complicated series of path
Laconic	Using only a few words to say something
Lampoon	To criticise publicly in an amusing way
Laureate	An official honour for personal achievement
Legislative	Related to making and passing laws
Martyr	One who dies for a noble cause
Migratory	A bird that comes and goes with seasons
Maiden	The first important act
Monogamy	The practice of having one wife
Matinee	A film show in the afternoon

Mercenary	The motive to earn money
Materialistic	An attitude that takes matter as everything
Neurotic	One suffering from nervous disorder
Notorious	Having a bad reputation
Obsolete	No longer in use
Optimism	To look at the brighter side of life
Orator	One who makes an eloquent speech
Orphan	A child whose parents are dead
Omnipotent	One who is all powerful
Omnipresent	One who is present everywhere
Omniscient	One who knows everything
Omnivorous	One who eats everything
Patriot	One who has great love for his country
Posthumous	Birth/publication after the death of father/writer
Patrimony	Property inherited from father and ancestors
Philanthropist	One who does good to mankind
Pessimist	One who sees the darker side of life
Parasite	That which exists by living on others
Postmortem	Medical examination of a dead body
Polygamy	Practice of having more than one wives
Panacea	Remedy for all diseases
Prodigal	One who wastes money
Popular	To be liked by everybody.
Recluse	One who lives alone and avoids people
Reticent	Reserved in speech
Reformer	One who works for change for better
Reincarnate	To be born again in another body
Renounce	To officially deny to keep a position
Replica	An exact copy of something
Repression	The act of using force to control
Resort	A place for holidays
Retrieval	The process of getting something back
Sinecure	An office with no work and high perks
Soliloquy	The act of speaking when alone
Unanimous	All of the same opinion

Unambiguous	That which is not vague
Unavoidable	That which can't be avoided
Unimaginable	That which can't be imagined
Unknowable	That which can't be known
Unreliable	That which can't be relied upon
Unparalleled	That which has no match
Unusual	That which is not common
Unforeseen	That which is not seen before
Verbose	That which is full of words
Vegetarian	That one who lives on vegetables
Veteran	That one with a long experience
Wardrobe	Place where clothes are kept
Waterproof	That which can keep water out
Widow	A woman whose husband is dead
Widower	A man whose wife is dead

Trades and Professions

Actuary	One who is an expert in statistics
Bagman	One who is a travelling salesman
Cartomancer	One who is afortune teller and uses cards
Duffer	One who is a pedlar (of cheap goods)
Optician	One who tests eyesight and sells spectacles
Physician	One who attends to sick people and prescribes medicine
Druggist, pharmacist	One who compounds or sells drgus
Dentist	One who attends to the teeth
Chiropodist	One skilled in the care of hands and feet
Masseur	One who treats diseases by rubbing the muscles
Obstetrician, accoucheur	A physician who assists women at child-birth
Chauffeur	One who drives a motor-car
Engineer	One who manages or attends to an engine
Captain	One who is carge of a ship
Admiral	The commander of a fleet
Sculptor	One who carves in stone
Lapidary, lapidist	One who cuts precious stones
Journalist, reporter	One who writes for the newspapers corresponent
Compositor	One who sets type for books, newspapers etc.

Draughtsman	One who plans
Florist	One who deals in flowers
Drover	One who deals in cattle
Ironmonger	One who deals in iron and hardware
Herbalist	One who deals in medicinal herbs
Fishmonger	One who deals in fish
Furrier	One who deals in furs
Plumber	One who sets glass in lead esp. Mending water pipes
Stoker	One who attends to the fire of a steam engine
Cooper	One who makes barrels, tubs, etc.
Navvy	One employed as labourer to do excavating work
Draper	One who deals in clothes and other fabrics
Jockey	A professional rider in horse races
Geologist	One who studies rocks and soils
Archaeologist	One who studies the past through objects left behind
Astronomer	One who studies the stars
Astrologer	One who foretells things by the stars
Pilot	One who flies an aeroplane
Collier	One who works in a coal-mine
Tanner	One who converts raw hide into leather
Cutler	One who makes or deals in cutting instruments, elg., Knives
Scavenger	One who clans the street
Confectioner	One who sells sweets and pastries
Janitor	One who takes care of a building
Poulterer	One who sells fowls, ducks, turkeys, etc
Cashier, teller	One who pays out money at a bank
Upholsterer	One who makes and sells cusions and coers chairs, mortor-car seats etc.
Usurer	One who lends money at exorbitant interest
Cartographer	One who draws maps
Philatelist	One who collects postage stamps
Conjuror, prestigigitator, juggler	One who performs tricks by sleight of hand
Funambulist	One who walks on ropes
Acrobat	One who performs daring gymnastic feats
Grazier	One who pastures cattle for the market

Potter	One who makes pots, cups, etc.
Shoemaker, cobbler	One who mends shoes
Invigilator	One who watches over students taking an examination
Curator	One who is incharge of a museum
Librarian	One who is incharge of a library
Principal	One who is head of college
Mayor	One who is head of a town council or coproation
Pawnbroker	One who lends money and keeps goods as security
Auctioneer	One who sells articles a public sales
Undertaker	One who is a tradesman who manages funerals
Veterinarian	One skilled in the treatment of diseases of animals
Stenographer	One who writes shorthand
Poet	One who writes poetry
Novelist	One who writes novels
Author	One who writes books
Lexicographer	One who compiles a dictionary
Stationer	One who sells paper, ink, pens and writing materials
Ethnologist	One who is well versed in the science of human races, their varieties and origin
Anthropologist	One who studies the evolution of mankind

Types of people

Fastidious	One who is difficult to please
Callous	One who has no sympathy
Credulous	One who easily believes
Gullible	One who can easily be cheated
Fatalist	One who believes in fate
Feminist	One who believes in offering equal opportunity to women in every sphere
Teetotaller	One who abstains from alcohol
Fanatic	One who is wild and extravagant in opinion particulary in religious matters
Stoic	One who is indifferent to pleasure and pain
Sadist	One who derives pleasure from inflicting or watching cruelty
Introvert	One who given to withdrawing from others

Extrovert	One who not given to introspection
Pessimist	One who looks on the dark side of things
Optimist	One who looks on the bright side of things
Atheist	One who does not believe in the existence of god
Agnostic	One who doubts the existence of god
Egotist	One who delights to speak about himself or thinks only of his own welfare
Altruist	One who devotes his life to the welfare and interest of the other people.
Dipsomaniac	One who has an irresistible desire for alcoholic drinks
Philanthropist	One who devotes his service or wealth for the love of mankind
Somnambulist	One who walks in his sleep
Somniloquist	One who talks in his sleep
Ventriloquist	One who has the art of speaking in such a way that the sound seems to come from another person
Ambidextrous	One who can use both his hands
Industrious	One who is a hard working person
Judicious	One who is a sensible and prudent person
Fugitive	One who runs away from the law
Alien	Oned who takes refuge in a foreign land
Kleptomaniac	One who has an irresistible tendency to steal
Biblioklept	One who steals books
Iconoclast	One who breaks images or church ornaments
Martyr	One who dies for a noble cause
Recluse, hermit	One who leds a solitary life
Novice	One new to anything
Zoophilist	One who is a lover of animals
Amateur	One who engages in any pursuit for the love of it and not for gan
Mendicant	One, who begs for alsm
Connoisseur	One, whois critical judge of art and taste
Mimic	One, who is limitates the voice and gestures of others
Numismatist	One, who collects coins
Obscurant	One, who is opposed to intellectual progress
Blonde	One, who is a woman with light coloured hair
Brunette	One, who is a woman with dark hair

Philanthropist	One, who devotes his service for of mankind
Misanthrope	One, who is a hater of mankind
Cynic	One, who sneers at the aims and beliefs of his fellow men
Refugee, alien	One, who takes refuge in a foreign country
Exile	One, who is banished from his home or his country
Volunteer	One, who offers his service of his own free will
Conscript	One, who is compelled by law to serve as a soldier
Recruit	One, who is a soldier or a sailor newly enlisted
Non-vegetarian	One, who eats on animal flesh
Pilgrim	One, who journeys to a holy place
Mendicant, beggar	One, who goes from place to place begging alms
Demagogue	One, who is a leader of the people who can away his followers by his oratory
Sophist	One, whose reasoning is clever yet false
Pedant	One, whose reasoning is clever yet false
Connoisseur	One, who has special skill in judging art, music tastes, etc.
Patriot	One, who loves his country and serves it devotedly
Prophet	One, who foretells events
Voluptuary	One, given to sensual pleasures and bodily enjoyment
Hypocrite, imposter	One, who pretends to be what he is not
Mountebank, charlatan, quack	One, who pretends to know a great deal about everything
Mimic	One, who imitates the voice, gestures etc. Of another
Interpreter	One, who can enable people speaking different languages to understand each other
Linguist	One, versed in many languages
Host, hostess	One, who entertains another
Protégé, ward	One, under the protection of another
Prospector	One, who searches for minerals or mining sites
Courier	One, who is a messenger sent in great haste
Contortionist	One, who is an acrobat who bends his body into various shapes
Misogamist	One, who is a hater of marriage
Misogynist	One, who is a hater of women
Emissary	One, who sent out on a mission
Antiquary	One, who collects things belonging to ancient times

Government Words

Autonomous	A region that is independent and has power to goven itself
Bicameral	A parliament that consists of two separate groups of peole involved in making laws
A federal	A country or system in which individual states make their own laws, but a national government is responsible for areas such as defence and foreign policy
Imperial	Relating to an empire (the rule of one country over several other countries)
Independent	Ruled by its own government, rather than controlled by another country
Multilateral	Involving three or more groups, especially the governments of three or more countries
Multinational	A state or country has people of several different national groups living in it
Multiparty	Involving more than one political party
National	Owned or controlled by the government
Repressive	Ruling or controlling people by the use of force or violence, or by laws that put unreasonable limits on their freedom
Sovereign	A nation rules itself
Totalitarian	Controlling a country and its people in a very strict way, without allowing opposition from another political party
Undemocratic	Controlled by officials or politicians who have not been elected by the people to represent them
Unitary	Controlled by a central government or authority
Anarchy	Absence of government
Democracy	Government of the people, for the people and by the people
Autocracy, despotism	Government by a sovereign with uncontrolled authority
Aristocracy	Government by the nobility
Bureaucracy	Government by department of state
Oligarchies	Government by a few

Plutocracy	Government by the wealthy
Theocracy	Government by divine guidance
Stratocracy	Government by military class
Autonomy	The right of self-government
Politics	The science of government
Revolution	A radical change in government
Referendum	To decide a political question by the direct vote of the whole electorate
Interregnum	The period between two reigns
Regent	One who governs a kingdom during the infancy, absence, or disability of the sovereign
Consort	The wife or husband of a king or queen
Census	An official numbering of the population
Statistics	Facts and figures
Absolutist	Relating to politicals absolutism

Chapter 20

Words of Daily Use

Words that are commonly used in radio, television serials, films, news, etc., have been listed below in the given table.

(a) What to talk about Television?

TV and film people	They use ----	The program may contain ----	Films & TV soaps and dramas may contain	Comedies can be
Anchor	Autocue	Replay	Action	Amusing
Broadcaster	Camera	Audience	Car-chase	Anarchic
Cameraman	Costume	Participants	Climax	Entertaining
Actors	Lighting	Background	Close-up shots	Farcical
Actresses	Locations	Music	Dialogue	Frenetic
Commentator	Make-up	Laughter	Flash-back	Hilarious
Director	Microphone	Clapping	Violence	Idiotic
Crew	Props	Commentary	Happy-ending	Inane
Manager	Scenery	Commercial break	Tragic-ending	Silly
Host	Script	Computer graphics	Comedy	Offbeat
Interviewer	Sets	Crime	Humor	Quirky
Narrator	Studio	Reconstruction	Intrigue	Riotous
Newsreader		Debate	Love-scene	Satirical
Producer		Discussion	Murder	Side-splitting
Reporter		Exclusive footage	Music	Slapstick
Researcher		Highlights	Pity	Wacky
Scriptwriter		Library pictures	Story	Way out
Sound engineer		Live coverage	Shoot out	Witty
Stuntman		New report	Accident	Zany

TV and film people	They use ----	The program may contain ----	Films & TV soaps and dramas may contain	Comedies can be
Stunt woman		Outside broadcast	Sound effect	
		Phone-in	Sound track	
		Satellite link-up	Special effect	
		Title-music	Stunts	
		Video-clip	Suspense	
			Sword fight	
			Trick photography	

Films and TV serials or dramas can be----		Current affair programs & Documentaries can be
Action packed	Moving	Alarmist
Atmospheric	Nail-biting	Controversial
Chilling	Poignant	Distressing
Cliff hanging	Predictable	Educational
Compelling	Realistic	Enlightening
Depressing	Romantic	Factual
Disturbing	Sentimental	Fascinating
Dramatic	Shocking	Hard hitting
Enthralling	Slow-moving	Informative
Gory	Spectacular	Provocative
Gripping	Spooky	Revealing
Grisly	Stirring	Shocking
Gruesome	Swashbuckling	Superficial
Hair rising	Tear jerking	Thought provoking
Harrowing	Tense	
Heart warming	Terrifying	
Inspiring	Touching	
Intriguing	Violent	
Melodramatic	Visually stunning	
Morose		

(b) What to talk about Hair?

Hair style	Hair colours	Hair can be	Hair is	Other words
Curly	Auburn	Back combed	Bouncy	Bald patch
Beehive	Black	Bleached	Bushy	Blue rinse
Bob	Blonde	Braided	Coarse	Fringe
Braids	Carroty	Crimped	Curly	Hair band
Bun	Chestnut	Cropped	Disheveled	Hair extension
Bunches	Coppery	Dyed	Fine	Hairline
Chignon	Dark	Flicked back	Floppy	Hairnet
Corn rows	Fair	Gelled	Flowing	Hairpiece
Crew cut	Flaxen	Hennaed	Frizzy	Hairpin
Dread locks	Ginger	Layered	Glossy	Hair ribbon
Flat top	Golden	Premed	Greasy	Parting
French plait	Graying	Plaited	Lank	Sideburns
Hippy braids	Mousy	Scraped back	Limp	Troupe
Page boy	Platinum	Shared	Matted	Wig
Peron	blonde	Slicked back	Neat	
Pigtail	Raven	Streaked	Receding	
Pony tail	Red	Tinted	Shaggy	
Pudding bowl	Sandy	Undercut	Shining	
Quilt	Silver		Sleek	
Ringlets	Snowy		Smooth	
Short back sides	Strawberry		Spiky	
Skin head	White		Straggly	
Wedge	Brunette		Straight	
			Tangled	
			Thinning	
			Tousled	
			Unkempt	
			Wary	
			Wild	
			Wind swept	
			Wiry	
			Wispy	

(c) What to talk about Food?

Food can be	Food can feel	Food can taste	Nice food is	Nasty food is
Burnt	Chewy	Acidic	Appetizing	Disgusting
Charred	Creamy	Bitter	Delicious	Foul
Dry	Crisp	Bland	Luscious	Un edible
Fatty	Crumby	Fiery	Moorish	Nauseating
Filling	Crunchy	Fruity	Mouth watering	Revolting
Fresh	Glutinous	Hot	Scrumptious	Unappetizing
Healthy	Greasy	Insipid	Tasty	Vile
Indigestible	Leathery	Peppery	Yummy	Yucky
Juicy	Lumpy	Salty		
Lukewarm	Musky	Savoury		
Mouldy	Oily	Sharp		
Nourishing	Rubbery	Sickly		
Piping hot	Runny	Sour		
Raw	Slurry	Spicy		
Rich	Sloppy	Sugary		
Satisfying	Smooth	Sweet		
Scalding	Soggy	Syrupy		
Sizzling	Spongy	Tangy		
Stale	Squashy	Tart		
Steaming	Squeegee	Tasteful		
Stogy	Sticky	Tasteless		
Succulent	Stringy	Vinegar		
Tepid	Tender			
Undercooked	Tough			
Wholesome	Wobbly			

(d) What to talk about Good Things or Persons?

A good person is	A good child is	A good deed is	A good work is
Blameless	Angelic	Altruistic	Admirable
Decent	Cooperative	Caring	Careful
Honest	Docile	Charitable	Commendable

A good person is	A good child is	A good deed is	A good work is
Honourable	Helpful	Considerate	Competent
Just	Obedient	Competent	Excellent
Kind	Obliging	Generous	First rate
Law abiding	Polite	Helpful	Pleasing
Moral	Well behaved	Humane	Satisfactory
Righteous	Well mannered	Kind	Sound
Saintly	Willing	Thoughtful	Splendid
Trustworthy		Unselfish	Thorough
Upright			
Virtuous			

A good mood is	A good film is	Good weather is	A good book is
Buoyant	Brilliant	Bright	Appreciable
Carefree	Excellent	Calm	Elucidating
Cheerful	Fantastic	Clear	Exemplary
Cheery	Great	Cloudless	Factual
Chirpy	Impressive	Fabulous	Gratifying
Contented	Marvelous	Fair	Illustrative
Happy	Outstanding	Fine	Impressive
Jolly	Sensational	Glorious	Informative
Jovial	Superb	Mild	Planned
Light hearted	Terrific	Sunny	Systematic
Optimistic	Wonderful		Valuable
Positive			Well presented
			Well written

(e) What to talk about Persons, Personality and Character?

Gentle	Admirable	Supreme	Competitive
Mild	Exceptional	Worthy	Solitary
Moderate	Marvelous	Qualified	Flexible
Temperate	Spanking	Wise	Rational
Kind	Splendid	Prime	Open minded

Genial	Sterling	Ace	Aggressive
Noble	Stupendous	Patrician	Courageous
Upper class	Eminent	Condescending	Impulsive
Well born	Wonderful	Patronizing	Ambitious
Superior	Sound	Advantageous	Careful
Excellent	Tip-top	Satisfied	Heedful
Dignified	Trimmed	Decent	Well-organised
Meritorious	Suitable	Fair	Imaginative
Virtuous	Aristocrat	Mediocre	Practical
Obedient	Respectable	Middling	Pragmatic
Decorous	Orderly	Passable	Sociable
Proper	Well-behaved	Tolerable	Stubborn
Egocentric	Well-mannered	Selfless	Intuitive
Secretive	Cautious	Organized	Carefree
Miser	Frugal	Extravagant	Balanced

(f) How to describe the features of a Man?

Height	Tall; short; lanky; of average height.
Weight/Build	Stout; chunky; skinny; stocky; slender; muscular; slim; tall and thin; short and fat; obese; impolite; heavy; medium; well built; broad chest; overweight; underweight; pear-shaped; broad shouldered; droopy shouldered; poised; slouched; balanced.
Facial	Black; red; white; dark; dark skinned; light skin; Caucasian; albino; fair; tan; olive skin; brown; double chin; freckles; (pimples/moles/spots/zits)
Nose	Ski-lope nose; pug nose; Roman nose; small nose; big nose; flat nose.
Eyes	Droopy eyes; big; ballooned; bags under the eyes; green; blue; ice blue; brown; hazel; blonde; brunette.
Facial hair	Mustache; beard; stubble; shadowed; thin eyebrows; bushy eyebrows.
Facial shape	Oval; chubby cheeks; round; square; long; apple shaped; pear shaped; conical; flat.
Teeth	Straight teeth; crooked teeth; buckteeth; braces; gapped; yellow white; nice smile; smiling; broken.
Ears	Small; big; large; gumbo ears; dirty.
Hair	Thin; thick; long; short; curly; wavy; balding; pony tail; bangs; braided; matted; fluffy.

(g) What to talk about Weather?

Hot weather may be	Baking; blistering; boiling; roasting; scorching; searing; sizzling; sweltering; torrid;
Humid weather may be	Clammy; close; muggy; oppressive; steamy; sticky; stifling; stuffy; suffocating; sultry;
Cloudy weather may be	Dark; dismal; dreary; dull; gloomy; gray; overcast; sunless;
Foggy weather may be	Hazy; misty; murky; smoggy;
Windy weather may be	Blowzy; blustery; breezy; gusty; squally; stormy; tempestuous; westerly;
Cold weather may be	Bitter; bracing; chilly; cool; crisp; freezing; fresh; frosty; icy; nippy; numbing; perky; perishing; raw; snowy; wintry;
Wet weather may be	Bucketing; torrential; damp; drizzling; hashing down; pouring rain; pattering rain; showery; spitting; teeming; tipping down;
Fine weather may be	Balmy; bright; calm; clear; cloudless; dry; excellent; fair; charming; soothing; mild; pleasant; still; summery; sunny; sunshiny; warm; inviting;

(h) What to talk about Beautiful People and Things?

Women	Music	Weather	Scenery
Alluring	Bewitching	Brilliant	Awe inspiring
Attractive	Captivating	Delightful	Breath taking
Dazzling	Divine	Fabulous	Glorious
Fetching	Enchanting	Fair	Impressive
Good looking	Entrancing	Fine	Magnificent
Gorgeous	Exquisite	Glorious	Marvelous
Lovely	Glorious	Lovely	Picturesque
Pretty	Haunting	Magnificent	Spectacular
Radiant	Heavenly	Marvelous	Striking
Ravishing	Inspiring	Perfect	Stunning
Striking	Lovely	Pleasant	Superb
Stunning	Magnificent	Provocative	Wonderful
	Poignant	Soothing	
	Sublime	Supporting	
	Earthly	Wonderful	

(i) What to talk about Dances and Dancers?

Dances	Ball room dances	Dances can be	Dancers may
Ballet	Cha-cha-cha	Acrobatic	Boogie
Ball room	Foxtrot	Agile	Bop
Belly dancing	Jive	Athletic	Dart
Body popping	Quick step	Ballet-like	Glide
Break dancing	Rumba	Clumsy	Gyrate
Mod dancing, modern	Samba	Dainty	Hop
Pop dance, popular	Tango	Elegant	Jiggle
Country dance	Waltz	Energetic	Jive
Disco	(Other dances)	Expressive	Kick
Flamenco	Cancan	Exuberant	Leap
Folk dance	Conga	Graceful	Pogo
(Highland fling;	Hockey-cockeye	Lithe	Prance
Hornpipe;	Jitter bug	Lively	Rock
Jig;	Minuet	Lumbering	Shuffle
Reel)	Polka	Nimble	Skip
Formation	Twist	Poised	Slide
Hip-hop		Rhythmic	Spin
Jazz dance		Skilful	Spring
Latin American		Sprightly	Stomp
Limbo dancing		Stately	Stretch
Old time dance		Supple	Strut
Rock n roll			Sway
Square dancing			Swivel
Tap dancing			Teeter
			Totter
			Twist
			Twirl
			Whirl
			Wiggle

(j) What to talk about Travels?

Needs in journey	One may feel	Travel can be	Can travel by
Ticket	Nervous	Boring	Air plane
Boarding pass	Nausea	Bumpy	Air liner
Foreign currency	Sickness	Dramatic	Executive jet
Hand luggage	Excited	Eventful	Helicopter
Luggage	Exhausted	Exhilarating	Jumbo jet
Map	Fed up	Fascinating	Light aircraft

Needs in journey	One may feel	Travel can be	Can travel by
Passport	Tired	Nerve racing	Rail
Visa	Fidgety	Relaxing	Express train
Phrase book	Hot	Pleasant	Metro train
Travel games	Jet lagged	Tiresome	Bus
Traveler's cheque	Inertia	Rough	Car
ATM Card	Jittery	Smooth	Jeep
	Queasy	Tedious	Pick up
	Restless	Thrilling	Bike
	Sticky	Tiring	Cart
	Sweaty	Turbulent	Tonga
	Travel sick		Ship
	Worn out		Cruiser

(k) What to talk about Air Travel?

Airports have	Planes	On the plane	Problems in plane
Air traffic control	Ascend	Air steward	Air pockets
Tower	Bank	Aisle	Bad weather
Arrival halls	Circle	Captain	Cancelled flight
Bureau de change	Climb	Emergency exit	Delayed flight
Check in desk	Cruise	Flight deck	Lost luggage
Customs	Descend	Fold way table	Turbulence
Departure lounge	Drop	Galley (Kitchen)	(Plane sound)
Duty free shop	Glide	Entertainment	Drone
Flight indicator	Land	Parachute	Hum
Board	Mount	Compartment	Roar
Information desk	Nose-dive	Life jacket	Shriek
Luggage carousel	Rise	Safety belt	Throb
Luggage trolley	Soar	Seat belt	Vibrate
Luggage check TV	Take off	Window seat	Whine
Observation	Taxi		
Terrace			
Passenger			
Terminal			
Passport control			
Restaurant			
Runway			
X-ray machine			

SECTION 3
FORMAL & INFORMAL WORDS

Chapter 21

American English

English has borrowed words from almost every language of the world. It is used in almost every part of the world, but everywhere with little variations. These variations distinguish the British English from the American or the Canadian or the Australian or the Indian English. In India, English shows the impact of both British and American English. Hence, it is essential to know the difference between the British English and the American English; more so, because computers contain and follow the American English.

The British and the American English differ mainly in grammar, pronunciation, stress, spellings and vocabulary. This covers all the important aspects of a language, hence, the difference becomes explicit. Yet it is not unlimited. British English is guided by *Received Pronunciation (Educated Southern British English)* popularly known as RP. On the other hand, *the English General American* commonly guides the pronunciation given in the Dictionaries of American English.

American English has retained the meaning of many words common in Britain centuries ago; as 'apartment'. In American English, it retains the old meaning 'a set of rooms' but in British English, this word refers to a single room.

The American English has changed the meaning of many words, such as 'billion' which means a thousand million, while it means 'a million million' in British English.

In American English, there are words whose meanings have been extended as 'graduate' which refers to the completion of any course, while in British, it means 'one who has obtained a bachelor's degree'. 'Senior' refers to a person of higher rank or who has a longer period of service to his credit, while in American English it refers to a college student during his 4th and final years. 'Engineer' refers to people who design and supervise constructions or manufacture of machines, etc., but in American English, it includes the engine drivers as well. In the same way, 'timber' also means caliber or, calibre (in British English).

For certain objects, there is one word in British English but another word in American English.

British English	American English	British English	American English
public convenience	comfort station	small sweet cake	cookie
exercise book	composition book	maize	corn
collar-stud	color button	biscuit	cracker

British English	American English	British English	American English
crematorium	crematory	chemist	druggist
made-to-order	custom suit	stupid	dumb
cyclist	cycler	lift	elevator
bowler hat	derby	engine driver	engineer
perambulator	baby carriage	autumn	fall
note (paper money)	bill	water tap	faucet
a thousand million	billion	ground floor	first floor
guard of a goods train	brakeman	goods train	freight train
visiting card	calling card	first-year at college or university	fisherman
sweets	candy		
coffin	casket	police constable	patrolman
cloakroom	checkroom	prison	penitentiary
shop assistant	clerk	full stop	period
cupboard	closet	veranda	porch
clothes-peg	clothes-pin	public school	private school
petrol	gas; gasoline	state school	public school
level crossing	grade crossing	railway	railroad
corn	grain	saloon (car)	sedan
football field	grid-iron	pavement	sidewalk
suitcase	grip	station master	station agent
pig	hog	underground railway	subway
bonnet	hood	braces for trousers	suspenders
caretaker	janitor	sleeping partner	silent partner
paraffin	kerosene	terminus	terminal
bank holiday	legal holiday	roundabout	traffic circle
number engaged	line busy	caravan	trailer
post	mail	lorry	truck
postman	mailman	main line	truck line
undertaker, funeral director	mortician	dinner jacket	tuxedo
		waistcoat	vest
receptionist in a hotel	desk clerk	ex-serviceman	veteran
nappy	diaper	waste-paper basket	waste basket
dressing table	dresser		

In British English, 'innings' is mostly used in its plural form, irrespective of the meaning being singular or plural, but in American English, the singular form of the word is used if the word is intended to have a singular meaning.

British English	American English
1. In British English, many words contain 'ou' as **colour, labour, vigour, fervour, flavour, honour, valour,** etc.	1. The American English has done away almost completely with 'u' from 'ou' as **color, labor, vigor, fervor, flavor, honor, valor,** etc.
2. In British English, numerous words contain 'se' or 'sation' endings as **cauterise, centralise, capitalisation,** etc.	2. But Americans prefer 'ze' or 'zation' as **cauterize, centralize, capitalization,** etc.
3. In a large number of words, the British use double consonants to give stress or emphasise on words as in **traveller, waggon, counsellor,** etc.	3. In these very words, Americans prefer to use single consonant: e.g., **traveler, wagon, counselor,** etc.
4. In many words, the British English has 'e' at the end: **calibre, centre, fibre, metre, scepter, theatre.**	4. In American English that 'e' occurs before the final consonant: **caliber, center, fiber, meter, scepter, theater,** etc..
5. The British have spelling of many words as they pronounce it like: **axe, plough, tyre, mediaeval, encyclopaedia.**	5. Americans have simplified it as it is normally pronounced: **ax, plow, tire, medieval, encyclopedia,** etc.
6. A number of words have '~ce' ending: **defence, offence, pretence, advice,** etc.	6. Americans use '~se' ending: **defense, offense, pretense, advise,** etc.
7. Words like **wheel, whether, where, what, white, whale, wheat,** etc. are pronounced with an initial, 'w'.	7. Words like **wheel, whether, where, what, white, whale, wheat** are pronounced with an initial 'hw'.
8. Words like **ask, dance, path, fast, last, cast, can't,** etc. are pronounced with /a:/.	8. Words like **ask, dance, path, fast, last, cast, can't** are pronounced with /æ/as in at, fat, rat, cat, etc.
9. Room is pronounced as /rûm/.	9. Room is pronounced as /ru:m/
10. 'tu' in the suffix '~tude' as in **latitude, longitude, attitude, altitude, amplitude,** is pronounced as /tu/in tune or tulip.	10. 'tu' in the suffix '~tude' as in **latitude, longitude, attitude, altitude, amplitude,** is pronounced as 'too' in tool or tooth.
11. Unaccented syllables are mostly suppressed. Last but one syllable is fully suppressed as in **laboratory, lavatory.**	11. Such unaccented syllables are given secondary stress. Last but one syllable is not suppressed, rather a secondary stress is given as in **laboratory, lavatory.**
12. Some words have different forms: aluminium, acclimate, candidacy, deviltry, telegrapher.	12. Some words have different forms: aluminum, acclimatize, candidature, devilry, telegraphist.

British English	American English
13. Compare articles: the day after tomorrow the day before yesterday half a dozen half an hour	13. Compare articles: day after tomorrow day before yesterday half dozen a half hour
14. Some prepositions differ: **in** Black Street **at** the weekends, **at** weekends stay **at** home a player **in** the team ten minutes **past** four twenty **to** seven write **to** me talk **to** someone meet some (no preposition)	14. Some prepositions differ: **on** Fourth Avenue **on** the weekend, **on** weekends stay home (no preposition) a player **on** the team ten minutes **after** four twenty **to/of** seven write me. (no preposition) talk **with/to** someone meet **with** someone
15. Dates are written in different ways: **23** February '**the** twenty-third of February'	15. Dates are written in different ways: February **23** 'February twenty-third'
16. Personal pronoun 'one' cannot go with he/she: as: **If one does wrong, one must be punished.**	16. Personal pronoun 'one' can go with he/she: as: **If one does wrong he/she must be punished**
17. When two syllable verb ends in '~ate', the stress is on the second syllable: dic`tate gy`rate mi`grate pla`cate pul`sate ro`tate stag`nate vi`brate	17. When two syllable verb ends in '~ate' the stress is on the first syllable: `dictate `gyrate `migrate `placate `pulsate `rotate `stagnate `vibrate
18. In British English, after 'seem' 'appear' 'sound' 'feel' or 'look' 'to be' or 'like' remains hidden as **I felt a fool. It appears a lovely scene. She seemed an expert driver**, etc.	18. In American English, at all such places 'to be' or 'like' is used as **I felt like a fool.** **It appears to be a lovely scene.** **She looks to be an expert driver.**
19. Present perfect is used for recent actions, especially with **just, already** and **yet.** **She has'nt washed the clothes.** **I have just seen the principal.** **Have you collected your gift, already?**	19. The Americans also use past simple in these sentences. **She washed the clothes.** **I just saw the principal.** **Did you collect your gift, yet?**

British English	American English
Present perfect with **ever** and **never**, not past simple. **Have you ever written a book?** **The bride has never seen me before**	With **ever** and **never** present perfect can also be used. **Did you ever write a book?** **The bride never saw me before**.
20. Normally, shall is used in the first person for the future. For stress will is often used. **I shall/will contact you.** **We shall/will attend the meeting tomorrow**. Shall is used for an offer or a suggestion: Shall I make coffee? Shall we go for a walk?	20. Normally, Americans don't use shall for the future in the first person. 'Will' is preferred. **I will contact you.** **We will attend the meeting tomorrow**. Should is used for an offer and would or how about is used for a suggestion: **Should I make coffee?** **Would you come for a walk?** **How about a walk?**
21. In Britain gotten is not used: **Your oration has got better.**	21. Americans also use gotten: **Your oration has gotten better.**
22. In negatives and questions both have not and don't have are used: I have not enough work. I don't have enough work. Has she got a web camera? Does she have a web camera?	22. Americans use only the auxiliary do. I don't have enough work. Does she have a web camera?

Origin of Words
Words taken from other languages used in everyday life

The list of words taken from other languages used in everyday life is quite lengthy, so a few of them have been sampled below:

Booze – Dutch	Banana – African	Jumbo – African
Zebra – African	Ketchup – Chinese	Shanghai – Chinese
Catalogue – French	Essence – French	Justice – French
Massage – French	Perfume – French	Regret – French
Terror – French	Tycoon – Japanese	Blow – Dutch (Germany)
Brandy (wine) – Dutch	Leak – Dutch	Luck – Dutch
Autumn – Latin	Dejection – Latin	Degree – French
Deposit – Latin	Depredations – Latin	Deodorant – Latin
Haunt – French	Merge – Latin	Merchandise – French
Mercury – Latin	Inspect – Latin	

There is a collection of curious and interesting words. Here are a few with their languages of origin and definitions.

Companion – It is both Spanish and French, but it has a Latin root, one with whom you would, eat bread.

Denim – French – The cloth

Victim- Latin – An animal that was to be sacrificed.

Worm – old English – dragon

Chapter 22

Headline English (Newspaper English)

Newspaper headlines are often *incomplete sentences*. They often contain a *noun phrase* with *no verb*.

Noun Phrase

A **Noun Phrase** describes a noun e.g. *exotic people*. Here are some examples of noun phrase headlines:

- ❏ Under pressure from Boss
- ❏ Unexpected visit
- ❏ Overwhelming response of voters

It is useful to ask oneself questions, such as, 'from what?' 'About what?' This practice helps the brain prepare itself by beginning to think about vocabulary related to the subject. For example:

Unexpected visits

The questions I can ask myself are: 'from whom?' 'Why was the visit unexpected?' 'Who was visited', etc. This practice of asking oneself questions helps the brain to prepare itself by starting to think about the vocabulary related to the subject.

Noun Strings

Another common headline form is a string of three or more nouns used together. In case of a noun string, its helpful to try to connect the ideas by reading backwards. For example, Mustang Referral Customer Complaint.

By reading backwards, we can guess that there is a <u>complaint</u> made by a customer about a referral program for Mustang cars, of course, we need to use our imagination for this.

Various Verb Changes

There are a number of verb changes that can be made to headlines. The most common are:

- ❏ Simple Tenses used instead of Continuous or Perfect forms, for example:
- ❏ Forgotten Brother Appease – a forgotten brother has appeared (after a long period of time).

- ❏ Professors prelist pay cuts – Professors are prelisting pay cuts (at the university)
- ❏ The infinitive form refers to the future, for example:
- ❏ The mayor to open a shopping mall. The mayor is going to open a new shopping mall.
- ❏ James Wood to visit Portland famous actor James wood is going to visit Portland soon.

Different Types of Newspaper Headlines

Straight Headlines

They simply relate to the main topic of the story and are the easiest to understand: For example

- ❏ Gurgaon's rain harvesting cost in demand

Headlines that ask a question, for example:

- ❏ Are hotels in shape for games?

Headlines that contain questions, for example: Mounties shot in arctic had no enemies at all.

Feature Headlines

Headlines of some unusual or amusing stories don't give complete meanings and it's often necessary to read the story to understand the headline, for example:

Two shot dead at Delhi Public School, NOIDA

Double Headlines

They are two part-headlines of the same story and are often used for major events.

Example: Militants hit U.S military chief plane in AF, Dempsey was not near aircraft during Talibans Rocket Strike

Headlines often use infinitives to refer to the future:

KMC yet to get MA history scores

(Kirori Mal Collage has not yet got the score of M.A history, first year exams)

'For' is used to refer to future movements or plans

More tests for students

(more tests are in store for students this year)

Auxiliary verbs are usually dropped from passive structures leaving only past-participles

Example:

Senior citizen, found dead in East Delhi

(Senior citizen a couple was found dead in East Delhi)

Articles and, verb, be are often left out in headlines.

HUSSAIN PAINTING OBSCENE, SAYS MINISTER

(The Hussain painting is obscene, says the minister)

In headlines, simple tenses are often used instead of progressive or perfect forms. The simple present is used for both present and past events.

BLIND GIRL CLIMBES EVEREST

(Blind girl has climbed the Everest)

The present progressive is used to talk about changes.

TRADE FIGURES IMPROVING

(Trade figures are improving)

While concluding, I would like to give the summarised version of the language of headlines.

Since headline writing is considered to be a very killed job, a good headline must:

Fit the story and tell the reader clearly what it's about.

Make the reader interested in the story and induce him/her to read on.

On the front page, particularly, the striking enough to grab the eye of readers, especially, at stations, newsagents newsstands, etc.

Reflect the newspaper's attitude towards the news story.

Fit into a very limited space.

Chapter 23

Language of Signboard, Notice Board, Ad, etc

Signboards are meant for general public. The following rules have been applied for collecting materials for the database.

1. The signboard must be the places in common public space and intended for a wide public.
2. The message must be directly or indirectly of illusionary nature, either explicitly expressing an order or a restriction or informing the readers of circumstances that can influence their action.
3. It must be non-commercial, i.e., it should follow public interest rather than that of a certain economic interest.

Analysis

1. Structure of a sign – some signs are very simple while others are longer and structured Some signs are called 'attention caller':

    ❏ Caution

    ❏ Danger

    ❏ Notice

    ❏ Warning

    ❏ Posted

    ❏ Attention

Characteristics of Signboards

An attention caller is invariably the first word of the signboard

2. Use of standardised formulation and constructions, these signs are standardised to a high degree so that they can convey a readymade meaning which can be understood by the reader without too much effort, e.g. 'No Smoking' and Do Not Enter.'
3. Use of non-text elements – On signboard graphic signs are sometimes used as logograms, i.e., they replace words or collocations. The signs used most often are in such a way, for example: wheelchair graphic (signboard) for disabled persons.

MEMORIAL HALL (Pictogram wheelchair)

Conclusion

Being straightforward in meaning and limited in the use of grammatical means, signs, notices and public announcements represent an interesting segment in the usage of English language.

Notice Board Writing

You must have seen notices pinned on notice boards in libraries or schools or any other place. Notices are written in order to inform the reader about some important information. A notice should always be to the point and short. A notice is always contained in a box. The common format for writing a notice is as follows-

Name of the Institution

Notice

Date　　　　　　*Title*

Content

Name

Signature

Designation

Please Note That The Capital Letters Are Meant To Be Written Like That And All The Word "NOTICE" Can't Be Changed

Now Let's Study Each Of Them In Detail-

1. **Name of the Institution**- It's simply the name of the institution on the behalf of which you are writing the notice.

2. **Title**-The Title should be short and to the point. If you are writing a Lost/Found Notice then your title would be as follows-
   ❏ ITEM NAME LOST
   ❏ ITEM NAME FOUND

3. Content-It should be short and straight forward.An average notice has 3-5 lines.It should contain the following things-
   ❏ What
   ❏ When
   ❏ Where
   ❏ Why
   ❏ How

   Please note that including all of these points is not necessary.

4. Name-Your Name Here

5. Signature-Your Signature Here

6. Designation-Your Designation

Characteristics of Notice Board Writing

A bulletin board (pinboard, pin board, noticeboard, or notice board in British English) is a surface intended for the posting of public messages, for example, to advertise items wanted or for sale, announce events, or provide information. Bulletin boards are often made of a material such as cork to facilitate addition and removal of messages, or they can be placed on computer networks so people can leave and erase messages for other people to read and see.

Bulletin boards are particularly prevalent at universities. They are used by many sports groups and extracurricular groups and anything from local shops to official notices. Dormitory corridors, well-trafficked hallways, lobbies, and freestanding kiosks often have cork boards attached to facilitate the posting of notices. At some universities, lampposts, bollards, trees, and walls often become impromptu posting sites in areas where official boards are sparse in number.

Internet forums are becoming a global replacement for traditional bulletin boards. Online bulletin boards are sometimes referred to as message boards. The terms bulletin board, message board and even Internet forum are interchangeable, although often one bulletin board or message board can contain a number of Internet forums or discussion groups. An online board can serve the same purpose as a physical bulletin board.

Magnet boards, or magnetic bulletin boards, are a popular substitute for cork boards because they lack the problem of board deterioration from the insertion and removal of pins over time.

Writing Good Advertisements

Always remember the following Ten Steps to write a successful Ad (advertisement) Copy:

1. Start by choosing a single benefit of your product or service that you wish to highlight above everything else. This is your "principle selling position" or PSP. To choose this, ask yourself what specific benefit makes your product or service different, better, or special. Is it the price, the convenience, the reliability, etc.

2. Write attention-grabbing headlines. This is very important. People are overloaded with information, so they skim read, particularly on the Internet. If your headline doesn't get their attention everything else is probably wasted because it won't be read. Your headline will often be based around your PSP.

3. Write a list of all the features of your product or service then translate each of these into a benefit for the customer. One way to do this is to look at each feature in turn then ask yourself "So what?" Imagine you're a customer; why should you care about this feature? Ask "What will it do for me?"

   For example, don't just say that you product is fast (a feature) tell the customer that it will give them more free time (a benefit). Better still, paint a picture of them using their free time to go to the beach, read a book, or relax.

4. Write the copy that emphasises the benefits in a way that makes an emotional connection. For example, let's say you're selling toothpaste. A feature might be that it contains fluoride. Sure, but that's boring. Rather, say it "Lessens Tooth Decay!" or even better: "Brush with Boffo and Avoid the Dentist's Drill!" See? You've turned a dull feature into a strong emotional benefit linked to people's fear of dental procedures. Isn't that more effective than "Contains fluoride"?

5. Start with your strongest selling points. The first few paragraphs are particularly important. Use them to create a desire for your product or service by briefly touching on the major benefits it will bring the customer. You don't have to go into too much detail up front as you can expand on these benefits later. Do try to get your big guns in early, though.

6. Testimonials sell. Good, believable testimonials from real people will help sales, particularly on the web where establishing credibility is a tough job. For even better credibility, ask your testimonial writers if you can include their contact details along with their testimonial.

7. Write with a natural style. Don't try to be pretentious or over friendly. Just write it the way you'd say it.

8. Decide who you're writing for and why. What tone are you trying to convey: light hearted, or serious? What level of jargon are you going to employ? Suit your language to your intended audience.

9. The final sales pitch, when it comes, must have three specific parts:

   It must incorporate a good deal; e.g. "40% off!"

   It must be urgent; e.g. "Only seven more days!"

   It must be risk free; e.g. "Backed by a 90-day, no-questions-asked, money-back guarantee!"

10. End by telling the reader what to do; e.g. "Ring now" or "Click here to order now for immediate delivery!" Needless to say, ordering details must be clearly visible and simple to follow.

Looking at these tips, it may seem that good advertising involves manipulating the emotions of your customers. Yes, it does.

Selling is a blatant form of emotional manipulation that involves convincing your customer that they want to buy your product or service, and they want to do it now.

Is this unethical? Well, it can be. It depends where you draw the line. In point 9 I said that your sales message must include a sense of urgency. A common ploy on the web is to include a claim like "Offer closes this Saturday". If you go back to the site the following week, though, the offer is still available. If you were tricked by such a claim, would you order from that company again?

So, by all means, use the 10 tips above to write as persuasively as you can, but remember that if you attract sales by deceiving your customers, you risk not only legal action but poor word of mouth, no repeat business, and more refund requests. So, be as persuasive as you can possibly be, but avoid the temptation to be "too" persuasive.

What's the Significance of a Good Ad?

Importance of Advertising

Today's world is a world of Ads. Whatever is displayed and shown to the public with good and relevant propaganda sales, whether it is goods or service! The package and display should be perfect and good to sale an item or service. Advertising is a favourable representation of product to make consumers, customers and general public aware of the product. It lets the potential buyers, general public and end users to be aware and familiar with the brands, their goods and services. Before going on to the importance of advertising, we would have an introduction to advertising first.

Advertising can be defined as a paid form of non – professional but encouraging, complimenting and positively favorable presentation of goods and services to a group of people by an identified sponsor. It does not include distribution of free samples or offering bonuses, these are sales promotion. In simplest words advertising is introduction, to consumers and general public, of services and goods.

Many people think that advertising a product means to sell it. But real aim of advertising is to make general public and potential buyers, aware of goods, products and services available under a brand.

Media of Advertising

Means communication by which advertising message conveyed to the audience is called 'Media of Advertising'. It includes both electronic and non-electronic means of communication.

Significance of Advertising

In a successful business, advertising play an essential and important role. Though advertising does not mean selling of products and services but it helps in increasing your sales. Advertising creates awareness in people. When general public becomes conscious to the products, services and goods under the brands, they persuade people towards these brands and make them buy better brands.

Advertising can be used to create brand awareness in general public and to make business more popular within the circle of potential buyers. Advertising, in a straight line, increases profit of the companies by escalating its revenue. The expenditure made on advertisement can turn as good boost in earnings.

Importance of Non – Electronic Advertising

This mode of advertising advertises brands via newspaper, pamphlets, brochures, magazines, journals and books. By this means of advertising, brands can let people, who are connected directly and indirectly with non – electronic media, know about their supplies. It also includes banners and posters. Non – electronic media is in reach of every locality. Advertising on print media is comparatively cheaper than advertising on television.

Importance of Electronic Advertising

Advertising by means of electronic means of communication is most the popular way of advertising. One can cover a wide range of audiences of all ages, color and gender by using this mean. Television viewers are in every home. *If one is advertising on TV* the brand would be introduced in almost every house.

Advertising on internet is getting more popular with time. It is the most viable platform available till date, for advertising, sharing news and creating awareness. You can get your advertising reached to every corner of the world.

Importance of Advertising Agencies

Many of the firms have their own department of advertising whose aim is to advertise the company's merchandise and services to the potential buyers and make general consumers aware of different aspects of their brand.

While, on the other hand, many organizations depends upon advertising agencies for promoting their brands and services which are available under their roof for the consumers' disposal. Organizations are supposed to pay a certain amount to these agencies for the promotion of their brand name.

Advertising agencies have expert consultants and executives to make proper strategies to promote your brands. They are always there to suggest, help and make most of your advertising cost by promoting your brand on right place, by appropriate means and at suitable time for apt duration.

Advertising, in fact, is proper promotion of the products not selling of items. By means of it organizations can give proper information about their brands to the costumers and consumers. Good advertising helps to increase sale and assist salesman to sale goods and services. It facilitates general people to buy advertised brands. Potential buyers are more interested in buying those brands which are advertised in an attractive manner.

Advertising can form a connection between the company and customers. It won't be wrong in calling advertising a means of communication between companies and their customers. Advertising does not give a proper awareness of brands but a nice introduction of companies as well. *Attractive advertising increases the demands of public which directly boost the sales of the brand.*

Chapter 24

Proverbs, Idioms & Idiomatic Expressions

What is a Proverb?

A proverb is most often a phrase or saying that gives advice in an obscure way. Basically, a *proverb* is a *popular* saying, expressing a truth or a *common* fact. Usually, a proverb is very well known because of its popular use in colloquial language. Following are some popular proverbs along with their meanings and usages.

"The best things in life are free."

We don't have to pay for the things that are really valuable, like love, friendship and good health.

"A stitch in time saves nine."

Repair something as soon as it is damaged. That's a small repair job. If not, you will have a much bigger and more expensive repair job later. Do it now and you'll need one stitch. Do it later and you'll need 9 stitches! (Why nine and not eight or ten? Because "nine" rhymes, approximately, with "time".)

"Still waters run deep."

Some rivers have rough surfaces with waves. That's usually because the water is shallow and there are rocks near the surface. But deep rivers have no rocks near the surface and the water is smooth and still. "Still waters run deep" means that people who are calm and tranquil on the outside, often have a strong, "deep" personality.

"He teaches ill, who teaches all."

The unusual structure of this proverb may make it difficult to understand. It becomes easier if we change the structure to "He who teaches all teaches ill." The word "ill" here means "badly". So it means that the teacher who teaches students everything, does not teach well. A good teacher lets students discover some things for themselves.

"You can't take it with you when you die."

When we die we leave everything on earth. We don't take anything with us. Even the richest people cannot take their money with them after death. This proverb reminds us that some material things are not really so valuable as we think.

"Better untaught than ill taught."

This proverb drops the verb "to be". But we understand: "It is better not to be taught at all than to be taught badly." It's better not to learn something than to learn it badly. This idea is echoed in Pope's famous line: "A little learning is a dangerous thing;".

"Don't cross your bridges before you come to them."

Don't worry about problems before they arrive.

"Soon learnt, soon forgotten."

Something that is easy to learn is easy to forget.

"Even a worm will turn."

Everybody will revolt if driven too far. Even the lowest of people, or animals, will revolt and hit back at some stage. Even a worm, the simplest of animals, will defend itself.

"It was the last straw that broke the camel's back."

There is a limit to everything. We can load the camel with lots of straw, but finally it will be too much and the camel's back will break. And it is only a single straw that breaks its back - the last straw. This can be applied to many things in life. People often say "That's the last straw!" when they will not accept any more of something.

"The way to a man's heart is through his stomach."

Many women have won a man's love by cooking delicious meals for him. They fed his stomach and found love in his heart.

"Where there's a will there's a way."

If one aims for something and one is determined to achieve it, one definitely does so and even God helps those persons who are strong -willed and determined in fulfilling their aims/goals.

"Marry in haste, and repent at leisure."

If we get married quickly, without thinking carefully, we may be sorry later. And we will have plenty of time to be sorry.

"One tongue is enough for a woman."

Some people think that women talk too much. If they already talk too much, they don't need another tongue. One tongue is sufficient. This proverb is another way of saying that women talk too much.

"If you wish good advice, consult an old man."

Old people have a lot of experience. If you want to have good advice or recommendations, ask an old person, not a young one.

"The best advice is found on the pillow."

If we have a problem, we may find the answer after a good night's sleep. People also often say: "I'll sleep on it."

"All clouds bring not rain."

We can rephrase this: "Not every cloud brings rain." And that's true. Sometimes there are many clouds in the sky, but it doesn't rain. Sometimes it's the same with problems, or what we think are problems.

"You can't tell a book by its cover."

We need to read a book to know if it's good or bad. We cannot know what it's like just by looking at the front or back cover. This proverb is applied to everything, not only books.

"Bad news travels fast."

"Bad news" means news about "bad" things like accidents, death, illness etc. People tend to tell this type of news quickly. But "good news" (passing an exam, winning some money, getting a job etc) travels more slowly.

"No news is good news."

This is like the proverb "Bad news travels fast." If we are waiting for news about someone, it's probably good if we hear nothing because "bad news" would arrive quickly.

"Live and let live."

This proverb suggests that we should not interfere in other people's business. We should live our own lives and let others live their lives. The title of the famous James Bond story Live and Let Die was a play on this proverb.

"Birds of a feather flock together."

"Birds of a feather" means "birds of the same type". The whole proverb means that people of the same type or sort stay together. They don't mix with people of another type.

feather (noun) = part of the soft, light covering of a bird's body

flock (verb) = gather in a crowd

"Tell me who you go with and I'll tell you who you are."

Similar to "Birds of a feather...", this proverb suggests that like minds stick together.

Idioms & Idiomatic Expressions

What are Idioms?

Idioms are words, phrases or expressions which are commonly used in everyday conversation by native speakers of English. They are often metaphorical and make the language more colourful.

Example:- Let the cat out of the bag : If you let the cat out of the bag, you reveal a secret.

It is important to remember that idiomatic expressions are used when speaking informally. They are not used in formal exchanges.

List of Some Commonly Used Idioms

Add fuel to the flames	If you *add fuel to the flames*, you do or say something that makes a difficult situation even worse.
	He forgot their wedding anniversary, and his apologies only added fuel to the flames.
All ears	To say that you are *all ears* means that ou are listening very attentively.
	Of course I want to know - I'm all ears!
Answer the call of nature or the nature's call	When a person *answers the call of nature*, they go to the toilet.
	I had to get up in the middle of the night to answer the call of nature.
Backseat driver	A passenger in a car who gives unwanted advice to the driver is called a backseat driver.
	I can't stand backseat drivers like my mother-in-law!
Badger someone	If you *badger someone* into doing something, you persistently nag or pester them until you obtain what you want.
	Sophie badgered her parents into buying her a new computer.
Balancing act	When you try to satisfy two or more people or groups who have different needs, and keep everyone happy, you perform a *balancing act*.
	Many people, especially women, have to perform a balancing act between work and family.
Bare your heart / soul	If you *bare you soul* (or heart) to someone, you reveal your innermost thoughts and feelings to them.
	Mike couldn't keep things to himself any longer. He decided to bare his soul to his best friend.
Bark up wrong tree	A person who is *barking up the wrong tree* is doing the wrong thing, because their beliefs or ideas are incorrect or mistaken.
	The police are barking up the wrong tree if they think Joey stole the car - he can't drive!
Beat a (hasty) retreat	Someone who *beats a (hasty) retreat* runs away or goes back hurriedly to avoid a dangerous or difficult situation.
	The thief beat a hasty retreat as soon as he saw the security officer.
One's best bet	The action most likely to succeed is called one's *best bet*.
	Your best bet would be to try calling him at home.

Bide your time	If you *bide your time*, you wait for a good opportunity to do something.
	He's not hesitating, he's just biding his time, waiting for the price to drop.
Binge drinking	This term refers to heavy drinking where large quantities of alcohol are consumed in a short space of time, often among young people in rowdy groups.
	Binge drinking is becoming a major problem in some European countries.

Bird In The Hand Is Worth Two In The Bush:
Having something that is certain is much better than taking a risk for more, because chances are you might lose everything.

A Blessing In Disguise:
Something good that isn't recognized at first.

A Chip On Your Shoulder:
Being upset for something that happened in the past.

A Dime A Dozen:
Anything that is common and easy to get.

A Doubting Thomas:
A skeptic who needs physical or personal evidence in order to believe something.

A Drop in the Bucket:
A very small part of something big or whole.

A Fool And His Money Are Easily Parted:
It's easy for a foolish person to lose his/her money.

A House Divided Against Itself Cannot Stand:
Everyone involved must unify and function together or it will not work out.

A Leopard Can't Change His Spots:
You cannot change who you are.

A Penny Saved Is A Penny Earned:
By not spending money, you are saving money (little by little).

A Picture Paints a Thousand Words:
A visual presentation is far more descriptive than words.

A Piece of Cake:
A task that can be accomplished very easily.

A Slap on the Wrist:
A very mild punishment.

A Taste Of Your Own Medicine:
When you are mistreated the same way you mistreat others.

A Toss-Up:
A result that is still unclear and can go either way.

Actions Speak Louder Than Words:
It's better to actually do something than just talk about it.

Add Fuel To The Fire:
Whenever something is done to make a bad situation even worse than it is.

Against The Clock:
Rushed and short on time.

All Bark And No Bite:
When someone is threatening and/or aggressive but not willing to engage in a fight.

All Greek to me:
Meaningless and incomprehensible like someone who cannot read, speak, or understand any of the Greek language would be.

All In The Same Boat:
When everyone is facing the same challenges.

An Arm And A Leg:
Very expensive. A large amount of money.

An Axe To Grind:
To have a dispute with someone.

Apple of My Eye:
Someone who is cherished above all others.

As High As A Kite:
Anything that is high up in the sky.

At The Drop Of A Hat:
Willing to do something immediately.

Back To Square One:
Having to start all over again.

Back To The Drawing Board:
When an attempt fails and it's time to start all over.

Baker's Dozen:
Thirteen.

Beat A Dead Horse:
To force an issue that has already ended.

Beating Around The Bush:
Avoiding the main topic. Not speaking directly about the issue.

Bend Over Backwards:
Do whatever it takes to help. Willing to do anything.

Between A Rock And A Hard Place:
Stuck between two very bad options.

Bite Off More Than You Can Chew:
To take on a task that is way to big.

Bite Your Tongue:
To avoid talking.

Blood Is Thicker Than Water:
The family bond is closer than anything else.

Blue Moon:
A rare event or occurance.

Break A Leg:
A superstitious way to say 'good luck' without saying 'good luck', but rather the opposite.

Buy A Lemon:
To purchase a vehicle that constantly gives problems or stops running after you drive it away.

Can't Cut The Mustard :
Someone who isn't adequate enough to compete or participate.

Cast Iron Stomach:
Someone who has no problems, complications or ill effects with eating anything or drinking anything.

Charley Horse:
Stiffness in the leg / A leg cramp.

Chew someone out:
Verbally scold someone.

Chip on his Shoulder:
Angry today about something that occured in the past.

Chow Down:
To eat.

Close but no Cigar:
To be very near and almost accomplish a goal, but fall short.

Cock and Bull Story:
An unbelievable tale.

Come Hell Or High Water:
Any difficult situation or obstacle.

Crack Someone Up:
To make someone laugh.

Cross Your Fingers:
To hope that something happens the way you want it to.

Cry Over Spilt Milk:
When you complain about a loss from the past.

Cry Wolf:
Intentionally raise a false alarm.

Cup Of Joe:
A cup of coffee.

Curiosity Killed The Cat:
Being Inquisitive can lead you into a dangerous situation.

Cut to the Chase:
Leave out all the unnecessary details and just get to the point.

Dark Horse:
One who was previously unknown and is now prominent.

Dead Ringer:
100% identical. A duplicate.

Devil's Advocate:
Someone who takes a position for the sake of argument without believing in that particular side of the arguement. It can also mean one who presents a counter argument for a position they do believe in, to another debater.

Don't count your chickens before they hatch:
Don't rely on it until your sure of it.

Don't Put All Your Eggs In One Basket:
Do not put all your resources in one possibility.

Down To The Wire:
Something that ends at the last minute or last few seconds.

Drastic Times Call For Drastic Measures:
When you are extremely desperate you need to take extremely desperate actions.

Drink like a fish:
To drink very heavily.

Drive someone up the wall:
To irritate and/or annoy very much.

Dropping Like Flies:
A large number of people either falling ill or dying.

Dry Run:
Rehearsal.

Cock and Bull Story:
An unbelievable tale.

Feeding Frenzy:
An aggressive attack on someone by a group.

Field Day:
An enjoyable day or circumstance.

Finding Your Feet:
To become more comfortable in whatever you are doing.

Finger lickin' good:
A very tasty food or meal.

Fixed In Your Ways:
Not willing or wanting to change from your normal way of doing something.

Flash In The Pan:
Something that shows potential or looks promising in the beginning but fails to deliver anything in the end.

Flea Market:
A swap meet. A place where people gather to buy and sell inexpensive goods.

Flesh and Blood:
This idiom can mean living material of which people are made of, or it can refer to someone's family.

Flip the Bird:
To raise your middle finger at someone.

Foam at the Mouth:
To be enraged and show it.

Fools' Gold:
Iron pyrites, a worthless rock that resembles real gold.

From Rags To Riches:
To go from being very poor to being very wealthy.

Funny Farm:
A mental institutional facility.

Get Down to Brass Tacks:
To become serious about something.

Get Over It:
To move beyond something that is bothering you.

Get Up On The Wrong Side Of The Bed:
Someone who is having a horrible day.

Get Your Walking Papers:
Get fired from a job.

Give Him The Slip:
To get away from. To escape.

Go Down Like A Lead Balloon:
To be received badly by an audience.

Go For Broke:
To gamble everything you have.

Go Out On A Limb:
Put yourself in a tough position in order to support someone/something.

Go The Extra Mile:
Going above and beyond whatever is required for the task at hand.

Good Samaritan:
Someone who helps others when they are in need, with no discussion for compensation, and no thought of a reward.

Great Minds Think Alike:
Intelligent people think like each other.

Green Room:
The waiting room, especially for those who are about to go on a tv or radio show.

Gut Feeling:
A personal intuition you get, especially when feel something may not be right.

Haste Makes Waste:
Quickly doing things results in a poor ending.

Hat Trick:

When one player scores three goals in the same hockey game. This idiom can also mean three scores in any other sport, such as 3 homeruns, 3 touchdowns, 3 soccer goals, etc.

Have an Axe to Grind:

To have a dispute with someone.

Head Over Heels:

Very excited and/or joyful, especially when in love.

Hell in a Handbasket:

Deteriorating and headed for complete disaster.

High Five:

Slapping palms above each others heads as celebration gesture.

High on the Hog:

Living in Luxury.

Hit The Books:

To study, especially for a test or exam.

Hit The Hay:

Go to bed or go to sleep.

Hit The Nail on the Head:

Do something exactly right or say something exactly right.

Hit The Sack: Go to bed or go to sleep.

Hocus Pocus:

In general, a term used in magic or trickery.

Hold Your Horses:

Be patient.

Icing On The Cake:

When you already have it good and get something on top of what you already have.

Idle Hands Are The Devil's Tools:

You are more likely to get in trouble if you have nothing to do.

It's A Small World:

You frequently see the same people in different places.

Its Anyone's Call:

A competition where the outcome is difficult to judge or predict.

English Vocabulary made Easy

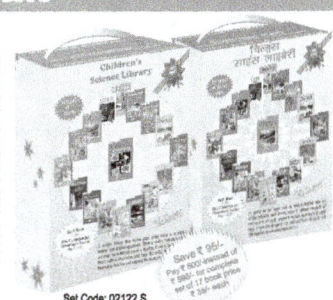